MY BALTIMORE LANDSMEN

Books by Herman Taube

The Unforgotten (Yiddish)
Remember (with Susan Taube)
Empty Pews
The Last Train
The Blizzard
A Chain of Images (Yiddish-English)
Echoes
Questions
Jerusalem — We Are Here
Between the Shadows: New & Selected Works
Land of Blue Skies
Autumn Travels, Devious Paths
Kyzyl Kishlak: Refugee Village
Land of Blue Skies (Yiddish-English)
The Art of Yankel Ginzburg
My Baltimore Landsmen

MY BALTIMORE LANDSMEN

A Documentary Novel

BY
HERMAN TAUBE

DRYAD PRESS
WASHINGTON, D.C.

Cover art: Yankel Ginzburg
Book and cover design: Sandy Rodgers Harpe
Photograph of Herman Taube: Nick Del Calzo

Quotation from Elie Wiesel's *The Gates of the Forest* printed with permission.

Published by Dryad Press
15 Sherman Avenue
Takoma Park, Maryland 20912

Printed in the United States of America.

This novel is available from the publisher and distributed in the United States and Israel at these addresses:

Board of Jewish Education of Greater Washington
11710 Hunters Lane, Rockville, Maryland 20852
Telephone: 301-984-4455
TDD: 301-984-1670 FAX: 301-230-0267

and

Beit Lohamei Haghetaot
D.N. Asherat 25220
Israel
Telephone: 04-820412

Library of Congress Cataloging-in-Publication Data
Taube, Herman.
    My Baltimore landsmen : a documentary novel / Herman Taube.
        p. cm.
    ISBN 0-931848-90-3 (alk. paper)
    1. Holocaust survivors—Maryland—Baltimore—Fiction. 2. Jews—Maryland—Baltimore—Fiction. 3. Baltimore (Md.)—Fiction.
    I. Title.
    PS3570.A86M9 1995
    813'.54—dc20   95-14826   CIP

Tell ye children of it
And let your children tell their children
And their children another generation.
— *Joel 1:3*

Dedicated to the memory of my sister-in-law
Brunhilde Strauss, of blessed memory
Born: June 15, 1928, Vacha, Thuringen
Perished: January, 1945, Stutthof Concentration Camp

When the great Rabbi Israel Bal-Shem Tov saw misfortune threatening the Jews it was his custom to go into a certain part of the forest to meditate. There he would light a fire, say a special prayer, and the miracle would be accomplished and the misfortune averted.

Later, when his disciple, the celebrated Magid of Mezritch, had occasion, for the same reason, to intercede with heaven, he would go to the same place in the forest and say: "Master of the Universe, listen. I do not know how to light the fire, but I am still able to say my prayer." And again, the miracle would be accomplished.

Still later, Rabbi Moshe-Leib of Sasov, in order to save his people once more, would go into the forest and say: "I do not know how to light the fire. I do not know the prayer; but I know the place and this must be sufficient."

Then it fell to Rabbi Israel of Rizhyn to overcome misfortune. Sitting in his armchair, his head in his hands, he spoke to God: "I am unable to light the fire and I do not know the prayer; I cannot even find the place in the forest. All I can do is to tell the story, and this must be sufficient." And it was sufficient. God made man because He loves stories.

— Elie Wiesel
The Gates of the Forest

Foreword

Baltimore was once known as the "Monumental City" and is still called "Charm City." Founded in 1729 and named after Charles Calvert, fifth lord of Baltimore, the city became home for people of many nations. The Inner Harbor became an debarkation port for immigrants from many lands, among them European Jews. In 1845, Lloyd Street Synagogue was the first synagogue to be built in Baltimore. The Jewish population grew from about 1,200 in 1845 to approximately 110,000 in 1969.

Of the total of 4,800,000 refugees who arrived in the United States between 1933 and 1948, 350,000 were Jewish. the Jewish community of Baltimore absorbed some 7,500 immigrants, mostly Holocaust survivors. They were helped by The Jewish Family and Children's Service, by The Hebrew Immigrant Aid Society (HIAS) of Baltimore, the Associated Placement and Guidance Bureau, the local branch of the Jewish Labor Committee, and by many individuals, both Jews and non-Jews.

The refugees were called New Americans. They contributed their energy and talent to the religious, spiritual, and cultural life of the community. At the Baltimore Hebrew College, in the early 1960s, 33% of top administrative and supervisory key positions were held by recent immigrants, as were 16% of all Hebrew teachers employed by schools affiliated with the Board of Jewish Education.

The New Americans were active as lay board members, staff members and executive directors at local organizations, hospitals, and synagogues. They were instructors and faculty members in institutions of higher learning.

Their contributions to commerce and industry in Baltimore was truly impressive. They became active as managers and foremen in the clothing and furniture manufacturing firms. Some of them climbed to lofty careers as top executives in insurance companies and partners and managers of local brokerage houses. Many survivors were self-employed, managing small grocery stores, tailor shops, laundries, photo and music shops.

This novel is based on the lives of survivors and their children, whom we call "The Generation After." I have changed the names of the characters and the names of the towns from where they came. But I used the real names of most of the Baltimore community leaders who helped restore our shattered lives, such as Harry Greenstein, Henry Turk, Dr. Eugene Kaufmann, Dr. Herman Seidel, Mayor Theodore R. McKeldin, and Rabbis Dr. Samuel Rosenblatt, Nathan Drazin, and Elimelech Hertzberg, of blessed memory. Their advice and encouragement helped them to start new lives in this great city. This novel is a belated and heartfelt "Thank You" for their untiring efforts on behalf of those who found sanctuary on American shores.

I sincerely thank Chaim Lauer, former Director, Board of Jewish Education of Greater Washington; Michlean Amir, Librarian, Isaac Franck Jewish Public Library; Dr. Michael Berenbaum, Director, Research Institute, United States Holocaust Memorial Museum, Washington, D.C.; Joy Gold, Production Manager, Board of Jewish Education of Greater Washington; Thama Metz, Irene Auvil, Beatrice F. Braitman, Shelby

Shapiro, Marc Breslau, Dr. Gail Malmgreen, Director, Archives of the Holocaust; Robert F. Wagner Labor Archives, New York; Vladka Meed, International Coordinator, Teachers Program, American Gathering of Jewish Holocaust Survivors, New York; and my editor, Merrill Leffler, for counsel and encouragement to write this novel.

I am also grateful to many survivors in Baltimore and Silver Spring, Maryland, for their assistance and cooperation in sharing with me their life stories.

I especially wish to acknowledge those friends, survivors and their liberators who helped bring about this novel: Chil Rajchman, from Lodz, Poland, now in Montevideo, Uruguay; Yitzhak Ginzburg, from Lodz Poland, now in Chevy Chase, Maryland; Jack Rubin, Baltimore, Maryland; and Sister of Mercy Josephine, Lodz, Poland.

H. T.

1

ON GARRISON BOULEVARD in Baltimore, Maryland, Sholom Schwartzman paced back and forth in the hallway of Beth Tefilo Congregation. Perturbed and agitated, he kept looking at his watch and at the door of the meeting room. There he heard a lovely clamor of women's voices, laughing, talking loudly, debating in a dialect so close to his and, yet, so distant.

The Rotstein Family Circle had invited Sholom to speak about building of a *"Shikkun"* (an apartment building) in Kiryat Siegal, in Ramat Gan, Israel. The plan was to house *landsmen* from the town of Smorodna, survivors of the Holocaust in Europe and of the gulags in Siberia. The apartment building would be named in memory of the *shtetl* and the people of Smorodna who perished in the Holocaust.

The Family Circle was named after Ozer Rotstein and his wife Sarah-Leah. Both were immigrants from Smorodna who arrived in Baltimore after World War I with four small children. Reb Ozer made his living by trading in souvenirs, relics, trophies, and emblems for tourists and military agencies. Later, he went into the wholesale business, exporting and importing toys from Hong Kong and Japan.

Reb Ozer gave his sons a Jewish Day School education at the Baltimore Talmudical Academy. His daughters were enrolled in the Bais Yaakov School for Girls. He married them off to fine young men and women from the Baltimore Orthodox elite. All children were active members of the congregation. They were ardent supporters of the Talmudical Academy, the Bais Yaakov School for Girls, the Associated Jewish Charities, and many other philanthropic institutions.

After Reb Ozer and Sarah-Leah passed away, the children founded a Charitable Foundation and Family Circle named after their parents. They continued to give generously to charity, and met bi-monthly at Beth Tefilo with their growing family members and some *landsmen* (compatriots) from Smorodna. There they enjoyed afternoons and evenings of family gossip and just plain togetherness.

♦ ♦ ♦

Sholom Schwartzman knew very little about the Rotstein Circle. When he arrived in Baltimore in 1948 from the Displaced Persons Camps in Germany he visited Reb Ozer to thank him. Reb Ozer had sent him, through HIAS of Baltimore, a document guaranteeing that he would not become a "public burden," and that he would also guarantee housing and employment. Reb Ozer greeted him as a friend and inquired about Smorodna. He wanted to know who had survived and what was left of the *shtetl*. He promised to make some calls to find Sholom a job.

"Call me anytime if you need help. I will talk to my sons and see what we can do for you, my dear *landsman.*"

Sholom did not need Reb Ozer's help. The director of HIAS, Dr. Eugene Kaufmann, and the Baltimore Bureau

for Job Placement found him employment at the Komfi
Factory. There he learned the art of designing bedspreads,
slipcovers, and curtains. Four nights a week, Sholom attended night school, studying English intensely. He bought
himself some decent clothes. Sadness remaining from the
camps gradually disappeared. He became more outgoing
and friendly, began to attend programs at the Jewish Community Center and dating girls whom he met at the shows
and concerts held there. In the evenings, in his rented room,
he read about America, Israel, and the Holocaust. He knew
very little about the war years because he had been isolated
in Treblinka and, subsequently, in hiding in Warsaw.

His new friends spoke to Sholom about meeting eli-
gible girls, thinking seriously about settling down, getting
married, and having a family. Sholom ignored all the offers
and the well-meaning advice of his friends. He hoped that
his girlfriend, Chanele, whom he had left in Smorodna
when he escaped, was still alive somewhere. Perhaps she
longed for and missed him as much as he missed and
dreamed about her.

He advertised in newspapers in New York, Warsaw,
and Tel Aviv that "Sholom Schwartzman from Smorodna is
looking for Chana Goratski and her family." He sent in-
quiries to the Polish Red Cross, to Yad Vashem, the Jewish
Agency, and other organizations. Weeks and months passed.
No answer arrived.

◆ ◆ ◆

At the Jewish Community Center he met Bettsie,
American born, shy and quiet, a gentle soul, humble and
soft-tempered. Her parents, Jacob and Emily Levinson, who
were also born in America, owned a furniture factory. Bettsie

invited Sholom to her home for dinner. Her parents greeted him warmly and invited him to visit again. Sholom and Bettsie began "going steady." They called each other every evening and she visited him in his room, helping him with his English homework. Bettsie stopped seeing her other friends, ended a relationship with Ralph, the accountant in her father's factory, and devoted all her free time to Sholom. One thing led to another, and one night Bettsie stayed in his room until it was too late to drive home.

The next evening Sholom asked Bettsie's father and mother for a few minutes of their time. "Mr. Levinson, I am a refugee from another world, from a different upbringing. Bettsie and I are getting closer and more attached to each other. Last night we talked until very late, and we did not want to disturb your sleep and call you. Of course, nothing happened between us last evening, because of my respect for her purity and innocence. But I admit to feeling a strong physical and emotional attraction to Bettsie."

He hastened to add, "I would like to ask you if you would accept me in your family as a son-in-law. I can't give Bettsie the comforts and luxury of your home, but I have saved enough to rent a modest apartment, furnish it, and get married, if you give us your permission and blessing."

Bettsie's parents had seen this coming. Bettsie, herself, had already told her mother that she had stopped seeing Ralph, that she loved Sholom and was waiting for his proposal of marriage.

Her parents, delightedly, said, "Yes."

Bettsie was an only child, and her parents gave her away in style. The wedding at Bluefield's, was attended by three hundred relatives, friends, and Holocaust survivors.

Bettsie's parents insisted that they move to a new home

in the Greenspring section of Baltimore. Sholom was offered a position as foreman-supervisor in the Levinson's furniture factory. He learned his new trade quickly, taking charge of the daily work assignments in the factory and warehouse. From foreman-supervisor, he was promoted to manager, working long, hard hours and doing his utmost to learn all the details of furniture manufacturing.

The harder he worked, the more his father-in-law, a man with a heart condition, was able to take it easy. He took his wife to Florida, to the Catskill Mountains, and on cruises to Europe.

Over several years, Bettsie gave birth to two girls and a boy.

After the *"Bris"* (the circumcision ceremony), Bettsie and Sholom were presented with a gift — a certified document that all holdings in the Levinson furniture factory and warehouse buildings were transferred to Bettsie, Sholom, and their children.

Sholom Schwartzman became a noted businessman in Baltimore. He donated generously to community charities and his name appeared as donor on letterheads of Israel Bonds, Histadrut campaigns, and HIAS of Baltimore. He was active on the boards of the JCC, his synagogue, and the day school his children attended. He was a good husband to Bettsie and a good father to his children.

Secretly, deep in his heart, burned a spark of longing for Chanele, his first love. He dreamed about her and saw her image, her thin figure, walking on the narrow cobblestone streets of Smorodna. It was all now part of a dream, a living memory.

◆ ◆ ◆

Bettsie had a steady maid and a nanny for their children. She spent her time visiting her parents, renewing her friendships, with former classmates, even with Ralph, the factory accountant now married to one of her friends from the Hadassah Club named Eva. She kept herself busy with the Parent Teacher Association and playing tennis with Ralph and Eva.

Bettsie was always home in time for dinner when Sholom returned from the warehouse or the factory. They talked at dinner about the happenings of the day, her parents' health, her tennis scores, and the children's progress at school.

Sholom seldom mentioned Europe, Treblinka, or the Holocaust. Every time Bettsie noticed an article in the *Jewish Times* or the *Sun* about Eichmann, about the discovery of new mass graves in Europe, she hid the newspapers and magazines. She knew it depressed him, making him moody and upset. His face would cloud with sadness and his dinner plate would remain untouched. Night would follow with nightmares, sullen estrangement, and silence.

◆ ◆ ◆

Bettsie and Sholom traveled to Israel for a Hadassah Convention. Bettsie was busy with the sessions and workshops, serving on resolution committees, and visiting the new section of the Hadassah Hospital in Jerusalem where a room was named for Bettsie and her parents. Sholom used the opportunity to travel throughout Israel, enjoying the blooming and growing Jewish homeland and searching for survivors from his *shtetl,* Smorodna.

Some of his *landsmen,* former partisans, camp survivors, and returnees from the *gulags* and Central Asian labor camps had made it to Israel and settled in fine homes and apartments, had good jobs, and were satisfied with their new lives in the Jewish homeland. Their sons and daughters served in Israel's armed forces and were becoming leaders in their new country. Sholom discovered a group of elderly men and women from Smorodna who lived in slums. Elderly people who survived the *gulags,* the *taigas,* they lived in old, dilapidated buildings in third-floor apartments on Joseph Hanassi Street in Tel Aviv. They were too old and sick to work and lived on meager pensions from Israel's Social Security Fund, hardly enough to sustain them. Sholom decided that he had to do something for them.

Upon his return to Baltimore, he called the National Histadrut Office in New York and set up an appointment with Israel Stolarski and Dr. Sol Stein.

Israel Stolarski, National Director for Projects, came to Baltimore and signed an agreement with Sholom that the Smorodna compatriots living in the Baltimore-Washington area would donate an apartment building in Kiryat Siegal (Ramat Gan) for the elderly survivors of Smorodna, in memory of the Smorodna Jewish community destroyed by the Nazis.

2

SHOLOM STOOD AT THE DOOR of the Beth Tefilo chapel, where his compatriots met. He was nervous, restless, impatient, and excited. This was the first time that he would talk to a large group of people in English. In his heart he felt a burst of energy, an inner satisfaction with the righteousness of his project. He was confident that he would succeed. He went over the prepared remarks in his head, the details of his plan which he would try to sell here to his Smorodna *"landsleit."*

The door to the small sanctuary opened and a middle-aged woman with a big smile invited Sholom to follow her. His heart pulsed faster as his escort took him to the pulpit, in front of the long, heavy pews full of people of all ages, all waiting to hear their guest speaker.

She introduced him by saying, "We have a distinguished guest among us this evening, Mr. Sol Schwartzman. He comes from our birthplace, Smorodna, and is one of the few survivors from our *shtetl.* He has just returned from Israel and he has for us a very important message."

All eyes were on Sholom; all were curious to hear what he had to say. With a flutter in his voice, Sholom addressed the group. "I am very nervous speaking to you tonight in

English. Please bear with me. It will only take me a few minutes to warm up and be more relaxed. After all, I am among my dear *landsmen.*

"I will try to answer all of your questions. But before I tell you the reason for my being here, I want you to know that I am now a citizen of this great, free country, and a member of this wonderful Baltimore Jewish community, thanks to your father, Reb Ozer, of blessed memory. Reb Ozer brought me to this country; he provided all the guarantees I needed to enter the United States. His was the first home I visited when I arrived here; he made the first phone calls on my behalf, trying to find me a job and a place to stay. Reb Ozer was not only a good husband, father, and grandfather, he was a *mentsch* with a warm human heart. His name will live in my memory as a man who touched my life."

With this introduction Sholom became a part of the Circle. The daughter and sons of Reb Ozer wiped tears from their eyes. They were overcome with an affectionate feeling of intimacy for Sholom, a man they were meeting for the first time.

"If Reb Ozer, *Olov Hasholom* (of Blessed memory), were alive today I would tell him that I met nine families, survivors of the Holocaust, who by sheer miracle came back to Smorodna from Siberia. They are our flesh and blood. They were forced to leave Smorodna because of renewed anti-Semitism. Their lives were in danger. Fortunately there is an Israel now and they were able to emigrate. Some of them arrived with only the shirts on their backs; some are old and sick from the years of hardship and tribulations in the *taigas* and *gulags.*

"I visited some of them in their little attic rooms, dwell-

ings not fit for human habitation. I'm convinced that Reb
Ozer would not rest until all our compatriots have a decent
roof over their heads.

"Unfortunately, Reb Ozer is no longer among us, but,
thank God, he passed on his good heart to his children,
who hold dear his legacy, his memory, and his charitable
soul. I did not come here tonight to bemoan our lost world.
I came here to immortalize your father's name, and ask you
to help me build a *"shikkun,"* an apartment building in
Kiryat Siegal in Ramat Gan, a home for our Smorodna
countrymen in Israel.

"I am happy to tell you that I have already donated the
first $10,000 for this project. I hope and pray that the
Rotstein Family Circle will follow my humble example."

A young woman asked for the floor.

"No one doubts the importance and seriousness of Sol's
proposal," she said, "but we donate every year to the
Histadrut Campaign. We already gave a substantial donation this year to the Dr. Blum Kupat-Cholim Clinic. Don't
forget that we pledged a considerable sum to the new
Talmudical Academy building. I suggest, therefore, that this
proposal be postponed for our next fiscal year."

Another woman in the back row raised her hand. The
chairperson asked her to come to the microphone. She was
in her late thirties, she was wearing a light blue summer
dress which fit nicely around her thin body.

Sholom looked at her gentle, pale face with no makeup,
her big, dark eyes, her hair sprinkled with silver-gray, and
something flashed in his memory . . . Chanele . . . but this
was not his Chanele; she was shorter.

The woman asked for permission to speak, and the
chapel fell silent. Even the teenagers turned to the podium.

"I will speak to you in Yiddish," she said. "I know that many of you here do not speak Yiddish, but I know that most of you understand the language of our Smorodna martyrs. All my years here I have kept silent because what I lived through in Smorodna would deeply upset you and give you sleepless nights.

"People ask me, 'Frumele, why is your hair so gray?' and I tell them that the images of our murdered children and their mothers, burned alive in our Smorodna *Beis Midrash,* follow me day and night. We worked digging graves for our dear ones. We were destined to be shot, and many of us were machine-gunned by the guards while running. But a few of us survived. Many are now in Israel, and they need our help. We must help them now. Next year will be too late for some of them.

My husband is not here tonight at this Family Circle reunion, but I pledge $500 for this life-saving project. I would like to assure my countryman, Sholom, that I will not rest; I will go with him to see each one of our *landsmen* and see to it that the survivors of Smorodna have a decent home for the remaining years of their lives."

The Family Circle voted to start the campaign immediately.

After the meeting, people surrounded Sholom and Frumele and looked at the architectural design of the proposed building. They offered him tea and asked questions about the situation in Israel. Some people asked for names and addresses of Smorodna survivors in Israel, offering to send clothes and food parcels. They invited Sholom to become a member of the Rotstein Family Circle.

The sad mood created by Frumele receded. People began laughing, speaking in loud voices, playing with their grandchildren. Sholom walked over to Frumele and extended his hand to her.

"Thank you for your help in my mission." He looked at her face, a face he had never seen before, but he felt a genuine closeness to her.

Frumele spoke to him in Yiddish, "I thank you for coming here tonight. I promise to help you complete this holy task. Please call me tomorrow so we can make arrangements to go and see some Smorodna *landsmen.*"

Sholom wanted to ask her where she had lived in Smorodna, where she had gone to school, and had she known a girl by the name of Chanele Goratski, but just then an elderly man approached, holding Frumele's coat.

"Sorry I came so late. They told me you made quite a speech."

"Mr. Schwartzman, this is my husband, Oscar Glazman."

Sholom and Oscar shook hands.

"Sorry that I wasn't able to be here earlier to hear your presentation, but I had to attend a very important business conference," Oscar declared apologetically.

"I am thankful to your wife for saving my project tonight, and it is really nice meeting you."

♦ ♦ ♦

Sholom returned home around eleven o'clock. The children and the nanny were all asleep. Bettsie was not home; she was still out with her friends. Sholom undressed, took a shower, and went to bed, but he was unable to sleep. Thousands of words and images came to his mind . . . Bettsie, Frumele, the woman who chaired the meeting, and Chanele

. . . begging, calling, pleading, "Please, don't forget me."

He was thinking that this Frumele, when you look at her from a distance, looks like an old, sad, suffering woman, but when he listened to her voice and looked into her eyes, he faced two burning flames. Her voice was so clear, her Yiddish so *heimish* (intimate), and he thought that if this Frumele would dye her hair like his Bettsie did, she would look much younger, like a real image of his Chanele.

Bettsie came home after midnight. Quietly, she undressed and crawled into their bed.

"Darling, are you asleep?" Sholom did not answer.

3

CHANELE WAS SEVENTEEN when she met Sholom at a meeting of Gordonia, a youth organization in the Zionist Labor movement. She was a an instructor and youth leader who played games with the young pioneer groups, sang, danced *horas* and lead outings to the forests around town where, around campfires, they would sing and share dreams of a Jewish homeland in Palestine.

Chanele was a charming, bright girl, interested in books and music, an easy-going, happy person, the only child of a well-to-do Smorodna merchant who sold accessories to the tailor trade.

She was a student at the *Tarbut* (the secular Hebrew language school system in Poland), and hoped to emigrate to Palestine after graduation, join a *kibbutz,* and continue her education to become a nurse.

Sholom was also an only child. His father, a master carpenter, was a very religious man with a deep desire for study. Every day, after eight or nine hours of work in his small shop, he devoted several hours to reading and Torah study. He spoke Polish and German fluently, having learned in order to converse with his customers, area farmers, and local merchants.

Sholom was an only son of Goldie and Joyne, their first three children stillborn during the depression years after World War I. Only Sholom, the fourth to be born to his mother, survived. His mother, weak from years of continuous illness, passed away at the young age of 36, leaving Sholom and his father, in the care of an elderly Polish housekeeper.

Sholom was given a traditional Jewish education at the Yavne Hebrew School. After school, he helped his father at his shop and at home with the bookkeeping.

After an accident which he considered an act of God, Joyne was left with an injured hip and shoulder, so he sold his shop, the machinery — the whole business to another carpenter, a former apprentice of his from Novidwor, and retired. He spent his days reading holy books, walking short distances with his cane to the *Beis Midrash*.

In 1939, his health deteriorated. He spent most of his days in bed, or walking around the house in pajamas and slippers, while Sholom worked as a bookkeeper in a local furniture factory and took care of his father at night.

Chanele came very often to visit Reb Joyne. She helped with the laundry, cleaned the kitchen, and listened to him chanting melodies from the Talmud.

Sholom agreed with Chanele that there was no future for young Jews in Poland. He was convinced that she was doing the right thing by attending nursing classes to serve in a hospital or clinic in Palestine. But as an only son, he felt that he could never leave his father alone.

Reb Joyne urged Sholom to marry Chanele and leave. He quoted the Bible, "A man should leave his parents' house and go and live with his beloved." You will not help my illness or my sufferings by remaining at home. Get married

and leave for *Eretz Yisroel.* We can afford to buy the certifi-
cate."

His father's selfless suggestion made Sholom even more
determined to stay. "No, Father, I will not leave you alone."

Chanele's parents were reluctant to let their daughter
leave. They preferred that she and Sholom marry and settle
in Smorodna.

♦ ♦ ♦

They waited too long. A cruel fate befell Poland. On
September 1, 1939, the German army attacked. After three
days of air raids, Smorodna was occupied by Germany. On
the first day, the local *folksdeutsche* and the German soldiers
grabbed frightened men and women on the streets and
from their homes, and marched them to the former Polish
Army barracks. Some of these buildings were in ruins, and
the young men and women were ordered to remove the
bricks and stones, as well as dead soldiers, from the collapsed and demolished buildings.

The corpses of the fallen Polish soldiers were hurriedly
buried in the dug out trenches around the former Polish
*Kazarma*s (barracks). The burial was difficult; people were
forced to dig mostly with their hands.

Chanele and her friends worked all day cleaning rooms
in the barracks and small cottages where Polish officers
used to live. In the evening, she was given a loaf of bread
and told to come back the next morning for more work
preparing the little houses for the German officers.

When she came home, Sholom was waiting for her, his
left eye swollen and his nose bleeding. He had worked all
day on the edge of the forest digging trenches and was

beaten by the guards.

Chanele and Sholom sneaked out through her back door and went to see his father. The front door was locked, giving the impression that no one was home. Jews were forbidden to be on the streets after 6:00 p.m. His father insisted that Sholom and Chanele take all the money in the house and leave for the Soviet Union.

Sholom did not argue with his father and left for Chanele's home. Her parents were hysterical, crying, "God punished us. We sinned by not letting Chanele go to Palestine."

He stayed for awhile and, in the darkness, left for his home, promising to return the next evening.

In the morning he heard howling. He looked out of his window and saw the synagogue on fire, devouring the nearby Talmud Torah building. The fire rose to the skies, and the autumn wind carried the flames to the nearby *Beis Midrash* and the *mikvah* (the ritual bath). Some elderly Jews were carrying Torah scrolls and holy books.

Soldiers on trucks arrived, surrounded the side streets and, with their rifle butts, pushed the elderly Jews back into the burning *Beis Midrash*.

Smoke reached their house, and Sholom's father wanted to know what was happening.

"Father, our *Shul* is on fire."

"Oy, vey! Did someone save the Holy Torah Scrolls?"

♦ ♦ ♦

After the fire, the daily arrests of Jews, grabbed from their homes and from the streets, continued. Civilian Germans went with the guards from door to door, telling the owners to leave their homes within thirty minutes.

Now Joyne insisted that Sholom leave immediately for Russia. He took his prayer shawl, his shroud, and the little bottle with sand from the Holy Land, and got dressed.

♦ ♦ ♦

"Judgment Day is here. Goodbye, my son. Escape as fast as you can. You can't save me, Sholom. Please leave. Save yourself, and take Chanele with you."

He went outside the house, leaning on his cane. The Germans offered him a ride on a covered wagon to a new home. Sholom was marched away with other men to dig trenches, deep, long dugouts, in the forest.

When they finished digging and had begun marching home, they noticed on the road a procession of covered wagons, followed by a column of soldiers on trucks. Minutes later they heard machinegun fire. By the time they reached the town, the covered wagons had returned, empty, followed by a column of singing soldiers.

There were no people on the wagons, only bundles of clothes, suitcases and prayer shawls.

Sholom knew that his father was buried in a mass grave, dug by his own son.

♦ ♦ ♦

That evening he went to Chanele's home. The house was already occupied by Germans, and a note was affixed to the front door: "House sequestered. Requisition by Military Command." A flag with a swastika was hanging from a window.

He went to the old section of the city, asking people who had returned from work at the former Polish barracks if they had seen Chanele. No one had. They told him that many of the men and women, after finishing their daily chores, were taken on trucks to other army barracks in nearby towns. Anyone who tried to escape was shot.

Sholom had no place to go. He began walking towards the forest. There were no guards stationed at the fresh graves. He cried, wanting to say *Kaddish,* but stopped.

No! No praise, no thanks to God. . . . Where is He, our Heavenly Father?

Although it was dark he could recognize familiar faces of men and women with carriages and wheelbarrows rushing toward the town. They had been told that it was permitted to enter the homes of the Jews who had been expelled from the center of town and take their belongings.

Sholom kept walking, and crying.

4

IN THE MORNING, tired and thirsty, he passed men and women carrying loads of vegetables on their backs. A peasant, driving a covered wagon loaded with bundles of straw, asked him if he had cigarette paper. Sholom said he did.

"Hop on!"

The peasant was travelling in the direction of Ostrow, a town away from the main road, seven kilometers from the nearest railway station.

Life in Ostrow was easier than it had been in Smorodna. Here he could still buy some food. He found a Jewish farm where he could stay and work.

But then one day the Germans came, expelled the Jews from their homes, assembled them in the market place and marched them off on foot to the town of Lubartov. Two days later they gathered all the Jews from Lubartov, Parchew, and the other small towns and villages of the area, packed them into cattle wagons, and shipped them to Treblinka. They hurried the people, flogging them with whips, canes, rods, and rifle butts, pushing, squeezing, one hundred and fifty people into a single wagon. Because this was not a scheduled transport, it frequently stopped to allow the regular trains to pass. The ride was hell, travelling all night, with no fresh air, no water, no place for the people to relieve themselves.

Sholom offered a guard money to get some water. The guard took the money, but never brought the water.

When they arrived in Treblinka, the transport waited for hours in a forest. Suddenly, the doors opened and all the people were ordered to get out in a hurry. Guards screamed, *"Schnell Ausschteigen!* Men to the right! Women and children to the left! Hurry out! *Rauss! Rauss!"*

The men were ordered to disrobe and to bind their shoes in pairs. Sholom and a few other young people were ordered by a German officer to swiftly collect the people's belongings from the spots where they had undressed and take them to a large place that was a depository for clothes, shoes, bags, and suitcases.

The men worked in a chain, running from the undressing spots to the receptacle. After he finished with the men's belongings, Sholom was hurried to the barracks where the women and children had been forced to disrobe. All the women and children were gone. . . . All that remained was the heap of clothes, baby bottles. and baby toys.

While running with the bundles of the women's clothing, Sholom heard a German yelling, "Who is a barber? I need barbers!"

Having nothing to lose, Sholom stepped forward, "I am a barber." Four men had already been chosen and Sholom was the fifth. The German told them to follow him to the clothes depository where they were given pants, shoes, and a shirt, and ordered to go to work, sorting clothes until they were called to the barbershop.

Meanwhile, the Ukrainian guards walked around with whips, continually beating the inmates, just for their own enjoyment. As soon as Sholom started working he got a beating. He was bleeding from his head and his face. He found some water, washed the blood away, and returned to work, sorting eye glasses, coats, and pants, searching if jacket collars, pant cuffs, or shoulder pads might be hiding any money or wedding rings. If he found anything of value he put it in a specially designated box.

He worked at this sorting place for several days and one morning a huge transport of new inmates arrived. Sholom was ordered immediately to the barber shop, next to the door to the gas chamber. The victims were rushed towards him, yelling and crying. They were forced to sit down, and he cut their hair.

A woman grabbed his arm, asking, "Will they let the young live?"

Sholom could not tell her otherwise, "Yes, the young will survive."

The woman said to him, "Now I can die assured that my son who came with me will live to take revenge for our tragedy."

Sholom and the other barbers collected the hair in boxes and valises, destined for German industry.

After five days in the barber brigade, Sholom was reassigned to Camp Two, known as the "Devil's Factory." Here he was beaten daily by the Ukrainian guards. One of the guards was called "Ivan the Terrible," or "the Devil-Man."

Ivan was a mechanic, a locksmith, who poured the poison gas crystals into the gas chambers. While the motors were running he walked around, beating people with an iron bar, obviously taking pleasure when the victims screamed from pain.

One day, Sholom was working with the Dentist Commando, removing false teeth from corpses brought from the gas chamber. The Dentist Commando worked close to Ivan's workshop. Sholom was working with a man named Finkelstein, an inmate from the town of Plotzk. Ivan came over holding a drill and stuck the drill into Finkelstein's side, laughing hysterically, while Finkelstein screamed in agony.

Ivan shouted, "If you don't stop screaming, I'll kill you."

This same Ivan would grab people and cut off an ear. While the victim was bleeding, he'd order them to undress, and then he'd shoot them.

There were two more evil guards, Micolai and one called Tzik-Tzak. All they did was walk around, beating and murdering people. Dr. Zimerman, the head of the Dentist Commando, would intentionally involve Tzik-Tzak in conversation, just to keep him away from potential victims.

In Treblinka, the inmates were not allowed to walk, but were always forced to run.

Sholom was always on alert, to guard his face from injury, to show no scars or defacing. He knew that whoever had a bloody face or a scar would be taken out of the evening roll-call line-up and shot.

Every day 15,000 people were killed, all of them Jews. Only one time did Sholom witness the killing of a transport of 500 Gypsies. The daily killing made him blind. He saw everything and perceived nothing. He became incoherent. All he waited for, all he hoped for, was that planes would come and bomb Treblinka, freeing him and all the inmates from their misery.

Months passed . . . years? He didn't remember what day it was. Life was worthless, the situation helpless, his fate sealed.

But, finally, the war turned against the Germans who

began to worry that the world would discover their mur-
derous deeds and the deep pits, the mass graves which would
prove their atrocities.

They brought in excavating machines to dig up the
bodies of the murdered people. Sholom and the remaining
inmates were now forced to remove the bodies of the victims, and burn them, 2,500 corpses at a time. The fires
burned all night, and in the morning they'd extinguish the
still smoldering skeletons. A specially organized "Ashes Brigade" removed the bodies and with wooden sticks beat the
remains into thin ashes.

Sholom was working in the *"Knochen* Colony," sifting
the ashes in special screen boxes. If he found a piece of
bone he had to beat it until it became as thin as cigarette
ashes.

The situation became so terrible that Sholom and the
remaining inmates in his command decided to rebel. On
August 2, 1943, under the leadership of two Czechoslovak
inmates from Camp One, they set fire to all garages and
warehouse chambers, and two hundred inmates escaped.
They were running in every direction, with the Germans in
pursuit with machineguns and dogs. Sholom kept running.
He decided to run alone, separated from the group. He
jumped into a deep ditch behind some bushes, in the opposite direction from the pursuing dogs, when he heard
salvos of machinegun fire, and then the Germans and their
barking dogs withdrawing.

He lay in the ditch until the next morning when he
noticed peasants walking on the road. Walking toward them,
he begged for food. Some said, "Get lost, Zyd!" But others
gave him apples, bread, carrots, and some coins.

He decided to walk in the direction of Warsaw. He

knew that his father had a friend, a customer, in Piastow. He even remembered the address because he used to write letters for his father and once visited Piastow. During the day, he slept in the fields and forests. At night, in the rain, he rambled toward his destination.

He looked like a living skeleton, and people took pity on him. One elderly peasant invited him to his *"chalupa"* (an old cottage) at the edge of the forest. His clothes smelled and his shirt was soiled. The old man asked him to take off his clothes, and let him take a bath and shave. He gave Sholom clean underwear, an old army coat and old army boots, as well as a hearty meal and enough bread and fruit to last him until he reached Warsaw.

The old man advised him not to use the main road. "If they find you, they'll kill you." Sholom thanked the old man for his kindness and help, and at dawn left for Warsaw.

He walked until he reached the Kostki train station. So he would not be recognized as a Jew, he covered his face with a rag, pretending that he had a toothache. When he arrived in Warsaw he took the tramway to Piastow.

His father's friend did not recognize Sholom. Instead, he thought he was a beggar and gave him a few coins. When Sholom told him who he was, Jarosz Waclawski almost fainted.

Sholom remained with him until the end of the war. Jarosz Waclawski provided Sholom with a document stating that he was a Pole by the name of Romanski who was employed by the railroad, a veteran wounded in the war, an invalid unable to talk. This document saved his life.

After Poland was liberated, Sholom returned to Smorodna. The town was destroyed, and all its Jews were murdered. He went to the edge of the forest seeking the mass grave of the Jews, the grave that he had helped to dig, but there was nothing left. Even the evergreens were gone.

He left Smorodna for Germany, and emigrated to the United States with the help of HIAS of Baltimore and his compatriot from Smorodna, Reb Ozer Rotstein, of blessed memory.

He tried to forget his past, but the images of his father, his Chanele, and his father's friend, Jarosz Waclawski, haunted him, in his dreams, at work, and even when he was with his Bettsie and their children.

5

THE NEXT MORNING Sholom left the house early. At the factory, he checked his appointment calendar, weekly project log, and material and supply requests. He signed some insurance documents, an order for a new assembly machine, and another for new fabric and yard goods. By the time he'd finished, it was already eleven o'clock.

He called Frumele. "Good morning. Sorry I'm so late. I had some things I had to take care of this morning. Can we meet today at two o'clock?"

"I can manage. Where?"

"At the Pikesville Deli?"

"O.K. Please bring with you copies of the drawings."

"Will Oscar join us?"

"He promised to help us, but he can't join us. He runs from meeting to meeting. I'll see you at two o'clock."

By the time he'd checked his mail, dictated some letters, called home and talked to Bettsie, it was time to go. He managed not to speed but still arrived in time. Frumele was waiting for him.

It was past the busy lunch hour, and there weren't many people in the deli. Frumele ordered a salad, Sholom a tuna sandwich. Both felt an immediate intimacy, like two relatives who hadn't seen each other for years and suddenly meet.

"I really must thank you for what you did last night. Providence sent you to that meeting."

"Leave Providence and praise out of our conversation. It is childish to think that I changed the results of your presentation by the order of Providence to attend the Circle meeting. I was there and did what I felt I had to do. I didn't do it for you, but for our people, our parents, our compatriots. Where do we go from here?"

"I made up a list of people I do business with, very generous people. I will call them and set up appointments to see them. I've also put together a list of Smorodner *landsmen* in New York, Elizabeth, and Miami. I'll call them, or write to them."

While they were eating, Frumele was mentioning names of people she would be glad to approach: Hoffberger, Meyerhoff, Levinsohn, Cardin, Epstein, Seidel, Libov, Skliar, Carliner, Landsburg.

"Some of them never heard of Smorodna, but they will support a project in Israel for survivors. Not to brag, but Oscar and I were very generous to their appeals for support for their favorite charities, so I hope they will respond to our appeal."

"*Halevay!* I hope so. When it comes to asking people to give, I'd rather write a check myself than solicit others . . . but I consider this campaign an act of faith. I feel we have a moral obligation to help the few who survived."

"We have some Christian friends, very fine, generous people. I would like to include them as prospects to be solicited."

"I'm not very much inclined to approach Christians to donate to our project. When I was in school, I studied about the Inquisition and the cruel abuse of Jews during the occupation of our hometown, so I'd be reluctant to ask Christians for donations."

"Dear Sholom, our friend, Rabbi Elimelech Hertzberg, says that charity is not the effect of faith, it is faith. It is the common denominator that unites people of all backgrounds and all religions. Charity is a great motivator for *menschlechkeit,* the bridge that unites people of all races, colors, and religions. I want you to know that the fact that I am sitting here, next to you, alive, is thanks to courageous Christian nuns who risked their lives to save mine."

"Really? Please tell me what happened. Share your story with me."

"Some other time. Come to think of it, Rabbi Hertzberg can provide us with a list of names. I will call him today."

For a while they ate in silence. Then Sholom said quietly, "You must have a very interesting story to tell."

Frumele gave him an awkward, sad look, as the words quietly and very seriously came tumbling forth, "Interesting saga? Hell, no! Tragic? Painful? Yes! And by the way, you asked me if I ever met a girl named Chanele Goratski? The answer is no, but I do remember that the Germans, during the first week they occupied Smorodna, went from door to door, picking young boys and girls to do cleaning work in the military barracks on the outskirts of town. Some returned every evening and some escaped, but if they were found, they were shot in the nearby forests. I hope she was one of the lucky ones who escaped and survived."

Sholom moved his unfinished sandwich away. Frumele said nothing, but put her hand over his. "It doesn't make any difference now, does it?"

"I still can't forget her."

Tears came to Frumele's eyes. "You think that you are

the only one? My whole family perished. I married Oscar, and he is a wonderful husband and friend. He is also a father to me, but the pain of the past, the memories, constantly haunt me, like a disease. The grief and bitterness of the past follow me day and night. I constantly ask myself, 'Why did I survive, and all my dear ones perish?'"

"We all ask ourselves the same question. Why were we spared?"

"During the war I wanted to live, to survive, to create and work. After the war was over, I had no desire to continue living. The war did not change only the Poles. I saw greed and lust, hate and envy, a whole array of crimes that made life intolerable. I worked with children who were in hiding. After the children were gone there was no reason to continue living."

"How did you survive the war?"

"We will talk about it some other time. It is not easy to talk about. When should we meet again?"

"I'll call you tonight, after I set up meetings with some of our prospects."

On the way back to the factory, Sholom had a crazy thought. "If Frumele dyed her hair, she'd look like his Chanele . . . and her Yiddish, her voice . . .

◆ ◆ ◆

The following weeks were full of eventful meetings, fruitful solicitations, wonderful discoveries of compatriots who lived in Maryland, Virginia, and the District of Columbia. They were filled with excitement, but also with disappointments.

Sholom and Frumele met daily, organized special parlor meetings, teas, and cocktail gatherings. He made speeches and she walked around among the guests, collecting checks, pledges, and envelopes of cash.

Thanks to letters in the Yiddish papers about the Smorodna *Shikkun* in Ramat Gan, checks arrived from all over the United States and Canada, from Smorodna survivors and their children. The Rotstein Family Circle became known in the Baltimore community because of an article by Maurice Shochatt in the *Baltimore Beacon* commending the Circle for having initiated such a worthwhile project.

But Bettsie was unhappy. Sholom was away every evening, and he was not spending as much time with the children as he used to. She realized that this venture was very important to him, that her husband was doing good work for Israel and for his landsleit. She was aware also that since he began this campaign his sorrowful demeanor had improved.

Especially pleased with this campaign was Oscar Glazman. Frumele was his second wife. On May 29, 1947, a United Airlines flight from La Guardia Field to Cleveland, with its 44 passengers and crew of four, crashed and burst into flames, in what was then the worst disaster in the history of commercial aviation. Forty were burned to death, among them Oscar's first wife, Sylvia, and their two children, Salky and Lazar.

Upon learning of the disaster, Oscar suffered a nervous breakdown. He withdrew from all his business and social activities, and, on the advice of his doctor, went to Sweden for treatment.

In Italy and France, he met some friends from New York, Jacob Pat and Charles Zimmerman, leaders of the Jewish Labor Committee. They invited Oscar to visit with them the Home for Tubercular Children at Brunoy, a sanitorium with facilities for the care of 125 children, and the Vladeck Home for Displaced Children in Paris.

At the Vladeck Home, Oscar walked around the play-rooms, the dining areas and the sun pavilion. He thought of his own children and his first wife, Sylvia, and then of all the children who had lost their parents in the Holocaust. A feeling of closeness to these children overwhelmed him and he thought, "Why not adopt one of these children and bring that child back to Baltimore with him?"

He turned to a teacher standing in the pavilion and asked about the little boy who was standing alone at the window.

"His name is Jacob. He came to us from a Christian orphanage in Poland. We don't know what happened to his parents. We know that his grandparents were deported to a concentration camp. Jacob suffers from depression and is a loner. He is one of my special students and receives extra attention. Otherwise, he is healthy and talented. He plays guitar and is doing well in class. May I ask your name?"

"My name is Oscar Glazman. I am a friend of Mr. Zimmerman and Mr. Pat."

"My name is Frumele. I came here from Poland with some of the children. I'm an assistant teacher, a block-mother, a nurse, a Jack-of-all-trades, as you say in America."

"Have any of the visitors who have come here ever tried to adopt a child and take him to America?"

"Many have offered to adopt children. Mr. David Dubinsky, a friend of my father's, tried to adopt Emily, this little girl you see here. But she has TB; she became ill while living in hiding in a damp cellar during the Nazi occupa-tion. The American consulate will not give entry visas to children with TB, and they require that people who want to adopt children be married. A child needs both parents. Does your spouse know that you are thinking of adopting a child?"

Oscar's eyes filled with tears. "My wife and two children were killed in a plane crash."

"I'm sorry I asked. . . . Please, forgive me. If you are serious and willing to adopt one of our children, go back to America, find a good woman who would like to take the responsibility of raising a war orphan. It won't be easy because these children need lots of attention and your undivided love. You can write to us about the child you like and we will make the arrangements. You can look forward to living a happy life with your new child."

"I don't know if I'll ever be able to live a normal, happy life after such an enormous loss."

"You can't go on living like this. We all lost our families, our loved ones, but, despite our experiences during the war, we go on living, helping children start new lives, a new future. By helping these children, we are helping ourselves. I died when I saw the remnants of the Holocaust in Auschwitz, the people, the images and echoes of the past. Their images still follow me, day and night. There are no magic formulas for survival; prayer doesn't help me anymore. Reality made a mockery out of faith for me. My life depended on sheer chance. Completely by accident, I was in the right place at the right time, and a nun saved me from the Nazis. Still, despite the pain and the memories, something in me wants to live, to leave here, to continue my education as a nurse, to serve children, to write, to be able to tell our story to the world."

"I've enjoyed talking to you, Miss Frumele. Can I come

and take you out for dinner, Jacob and you?"

"I must ask for permission from the director of the home. It was nice meeting you, Mr. Glazman. Please, come again."

6

Dear Sholom,

Twice already you've asked me to share my life story with you, but I am reluctant to talk about myself and what I went through during the war. Let me try to explain why I detest speaking about the Holocaust. First, even though years have passed since our loved ones perished, the wounds are still open, and the memories are still frightening, still vivid, and it's very painful and difficult for me to share my experiences without getting depressed all over again.

When I meet with Americans, Christians or Jews, it doesn't matter, I feel let down and discouraged, and I get upset. They don't want to hear our stories and, even worse, they don't believe our descriptions of the torture and the agony we went through.

They spent the war years having parties, celebrating anniversaries and birthdays, while our loved ones were being murdered. Even our landsmen *did very little to help their friends and relatives who were pleading for assistance before the onslaught. The more caring and conscientious ones raised money and gave to the Vaad Hatzala Rescue Funds, but they did very little to save us before the war, even after the Holocaust when we lived in the D.P. camps. In some Jewish com-*

*munities in Eastern Europe we feared every day that there
would be pogroms like the one in Kielce.*

*When I arrived in Baltimore, a friend of my husband's,
the manager of the Baltimore edition of the* Jewish Daily
Forward, *Mr. Henry Turk, asked me to speak to a women's
organization on behalf of the Children's Adoption Campaign
of the Jewish Labor Committee.*

*I'd never done public speaking before, but I accepted the
invitation, knowing how important the campaign really was,
to save these children, this remnant of the Holocaust.*

*Let me share with you some of my notes about my first
public speaking engagement:*

*The Hebrew Regal Society was meeting at a downtown
hotel. When I entered the hall, music was playing and
women were dancing, jabbering, and laughing loudly. I was
annoyed by the loud music and the outbursts of screams
which I wasn't used to. They tried to get me in a round of a
hora, but I declined the invitation. My cheeks were burning
in anticipation of my first speech in English, hoping some of
them would be willing to adopt a Jewish orphan.*

*The Grand Matron, in all her loveliness, introduced me
to the audience. My knees were shaking and I was holding
onto the podium as I started to speak. "It is good to be here
tonight. You all remind me of my mother. With a deep sense
of indebtedness to all of you who helped us come to America
from various lands to begin a new life in the Baltimore community, I come here tonight to share with you some life stories
of children who survived the gas chambers and are waiting
now to be adopted by women like you."*

*I started to tell them about my life, my parents, my de-
stroyed* shtetl *and the orphaned children whose parents were
killed by the Nazis and their helpers. I told them how these*

*children survived in the forests and were saved by the parti-
sans and by Righteous Gentile peasants, and were now in the
Jewish Labor Committee's Children's Homes in Paris, France.*

*The Grand Matron came up to the podium, "My dear
young woman, the war is over now. We don't need to hear
these upsetting stories. We can live without them. Start the
music, please."*

*I left the podium, grabbed my coat and left the hotel. I
jumped onto a streetcar and burst into tears. I never spoke
again about my life, except at the meetings of our Family
Circle.*

*I know how busy you are and I don't want you to sit
with me when we meet, and repeatedly ask me to tell you my
story. So I have decided to let you read some pages of my diary. I was naive after our liberation to think that the world,
our* landsmen, *would be interested to read about our town,
our lives before the war, and our sufferings during the Nazi
occupation, so I started to write my memoirs.*

*After meeting you and listening to you, I feel a closeness
to you. I trust in you deeply enough to share my notes. They
will give you my background and satisfy your curiosity about
my past.*

*P.S. My husband, Oscar, knows about my sharing these
notes with you.*

♦ ♦ ♦

*My father, Shaya Kleinbaum, was a tailor. My mother,
Rivka, was a seamstress. Both were natives of Smorodna. Both
had public school education and secular Yiddish schooling.
My father was very active in the Jewish Labor movement, the*
Bund. *He was a delegate to* Bund *conventions in Lodz, War-*

saw and other cities. I remember him receiving correspon-
dence from the Smorodna Landsmanschaften *in New York,*
Philadelphia, and Los Angeles, and also letters from Bund
leaders like Zivion, Vladeck, Chanin, and Dubinsky.

I was raised in SKIF and YAF youth groups. Later, in
Zukunft, *the social, cultural association for young people in*
the bundist movement. I was sent to the CYSHO school in
Lodz. I also learned Russian and English so that I could help
my father write letters to some of his American friends. After
the pogrom *on Jews in the village of Stawy and the town of*
Przytik on March 9, 1936, my father was arrested for orga-
nizing a protest demonstration in Smorodna, something that
had been banned by the government. Despite Jewish self-
defense and mass protests, 79 Jews were killed and 500 in-
jured in the violence against the Jews.

During 1937, there were further attacks on Jews
throughout Poland, and in Katowice bombs were thrown into
Jewish-owned shops.

At the time I was studying in Lodz, working at an or-
phanage, and attending nursing classes at Poznanski Hospi-
tal. At the hospital, they circulated a letter from Cardinal
Hlond, warning the Christian nurses and students to stay
away from us, Jewish students. This letter stated:

> "It is true that the Jews are committing frauds, prac-
> ticing usury, and dealing in white slavery. It is true
> that in schools, the influence of the Jewish youth
> upon the Catholic youth is generally evil, from a
> religious and ethical point of view. But let us be just.
> One does well to prefer his own kind in commercial
> dealings and to avoid Jewish stores and Jewish stalls
> in the markets, but it is not permissible to demolish

Jewish businesses, break windows, torpedo their houses."

Despite Cardinal Hlond's declaration, synagogues were desecrated and Jewish property destroyed, and Jews attacked and injured. Jews in small towns were driven to despair, discrimination grew, and stores and shops closed. Jews wanted to leave Poland, but the whole world was closed to them.

I came home on a two-week leave to Smorodna during the last week of August, 1939. Within a week, disaster struck. On the fourth of September, the German army occupied Smorodna. My parents urged me to leave immediately for the Soviet Union, as did many other young people. I was their only daughter, and I refused to leave them alone.

On the third day of the occupation, two Polish civilians with swastika arm bands and two armed Wehrmacht soldiers came to our home and asked my parents to follow them. I asked the civilians if I could join my parents, and they said to me, "Better not — stay where you are."

They were polite and promised that my parents would be back, after "an inquiry into their political activities in town." Hours passed and my parents did not return. I walked over to see some neighbors who were friends of my parents. Some of them had also been taken by civilians and soldiers. Others had been hauled from their homes by police and Nazi militia and made to clean the streets and buildings. They were beaten and returned home, half dead, after they finished cleaning.

Days went by, and my parents did not return. On the third day, when I returned from a neighbor's house, I found a note on our door: "House Confiscated, Seized by Order of the Military Commandant of the District of Smorodna. Owners,

international criminals, awaiting trial and sentencing. Un-
lawful entry will be punished."

Two heavy locks were attached to the front and back
doors of our house.

I went to the home of a girlfriend. Their house was a
mess, with windows broken and kitchen utensils, pillow
feathers, clothes, and rotten vegetables thrown all over. It was
raining and cold, and I was crying. I entered an upstairs
room, looking for something to wear. I was shivering.

Suddenly, I heard soldiers shouting, dogs barking and
saw civilians with swastika arm bands, running, banging on
doors, and shouting "Raus! Raus!"

I ran to the attic and watched soldiers chasing men,
women and children, herding them toward the Shulgas, the
Beis Midrash. I recognized some of our neighbors and friends
and some of my mother's relatives among them. I saw flames
coming from the old, wooden Beis Midrash building. I heard
continual shooting, an explosion, and, finally, everything fell
silent.

I sat there in the attic until nightfall, in total darkness. I
hadn't eaten all day, and although I wasn't hungry, I was very
thirsty. There was no water in the house, and the thought of
what might have happened to my parents gave me terrible
stomach pains. I went to the outhouse, rested for a while and,
when it was dark, went to the next house.

There, also, the doors and windows were broken, and
rain had poured in from all sides. I found some stale challah
(bread) which I chewed as I cried.

I decided I would leave just past midnight, even though
it was forbidden to be outside from 6:00 p.m. until 7:00
a.m. If I were captured, I had nothing more to lose. I knew
that in the morning the guards would come again, looking

for people who had escaped, and neighboring peasants would come with their carriages to look for things to haul off.

I walked quickly, seized by fear, but driven by a mysterious energy, like an animal pursued by vicious dogs. In the morning I came to a railroad station. Still wearing my nursing uniform and head scarf, I sat on an open train platform full of peasants, civilians, and some wounded Polish soldiers returning home.

A Polish policeman asked me for my travel permit. I told him that I lost my documents, together with my baggage.

He looked at me, "Zydowka?"

"Yes."

"Leave the train on the Zgierz Station. Don't get off in Lodz."

I said, "Bog Zaplacz (May God reward you)!"

He said, "May God save you."

At the railroad station in Zgierz, I met a school friend who gave me some bread, an apple, and one of her travel permits. She was employed in a military laundry of the German administration in Lodz, and was going home to advise her parents to leave Zgierz and move to Lodz. The Germans planned to make Zgierz "Judenrein" (free of Jews) by the end of the month.

The German population of Lodz knew in advance when the German armies would occupy the city. They knew who would be the first victims, as they had prepared a list of all Jewish industrialists, real estate owners, community leaders, trade union workers, Jewish writers, journalists, educators, and political personalities. As soon as the Germans occupied Lodz the arrests began. The sons of the local Germans, armed with ready lists and accompanied by German officers, started a daily, ferocious hunt for the Jewish leaders. They searched homes, taking whatever they chose, sometimes even taking the owners, who never returned.

Jewish citizens turned to their Polish neighbors for help, but the anti-Semitic propaganda poisoned the relationship between the Poles and the Jews. We were accused of causing all Polish misfortunes, including the crisis over Danzig. After entering the city the Germans let the Poles know that Jews would have no protection, that they were to be left to the mercy of a wanton fate.

Many local hooligans were waiting for this occasion and, with the help of some Dozorcas *(building doormen), they ransacked homes and apartments, insulting, looting, and beating any unfortunate people who remained.*

Most of the community and labor union leaders were able to leave the city and escape to the Soviet Union, although many trade union leaders were arrested and taken to the Radogosz Jail, also never to return.

When I tried to go back to my room, the apartment was locked. The owners, teachers at the Medem School, were gone. The Pan Dozorca *(housekeeper), a decent elderly Pole, told me that a German family was moving into our apartment on Saturday. "Better take your belongings before they confiscate everything."*

I took my small knapsack, my nurse's uniform, some documents, and school matriculation papers. The rest of my dresses, blouses, and a pair of shoes I gave to the Pan Dozorca. *Then I left my room and went to the Children's House. Half of the staff had escaped to Warsaw, and the home was a mess. The children were running around, unsupervised, crying and hungry. A Polish doctor and two nuns came and registered all the children and the staff. They ordered the Home closed and the children transferred to a Pol-*

ish Internat run by Sisters of Mercy.

One of the nuns checked my documents and asked me to step outside. I followed her to the yard.

"What's your name?"

"Frumele, Felicia."

"My name is Sister Zoshia. Do you have family or relatives here?"

"No, my parents were arrested. They were taken away, and they never came back."

"Felicia, you know what is happening here. Innocent people are being murdered every day. We have orders to save the children. We can use your help, and we can save you, too. Would you like to come with us, serving as a nurse and overseeing the children?"

"Let me think it over. This is a serious decision."

"Felicia, this is a very serious time we live in. This decision can save your life. Make up your mind. If you agree to come with us, I will have proper Polish documents ready for you before we leave. Our trucks will be here early tomorrow morning."

"I just want to say goodbye to some of my friends here, and see what they are planning."

"I hope to see you in the morning. Come with us. Help us save the children. And you will save yourself."

On my way to my friend's home on Pomorska Street, I was grabbed by German civilians and, together with a group of men and women, taken to the Etingon Factory. First we had to clean the halls, rooms, and toilets. Then they forced us, the women and the men, to undress, and to dance and to sing. "This is your Jewish holiday," they shouted, beating us with wet towels, wooden sticks, and rifle butts.

In the evening, just before curfew, the time when it was

prohibited for us to be on the streets, our sad group was told that we could leave.

My face was covered with soot and blood. My nurse's outfit was dirty, stained from a nosebleed, and smelly from the stinking odor of the chemicals I used to clean the toilets. I returned to the Children's Home, showered, changed into fresh underwear and a clean nurse's uniform, and a Red Cross hair cover.

I was not hungry, but bitter and angry. I was struck with fear and nausea, waiting for this night to be over, and for Sister Zoshia to arrive.

We left Lodz early with two truckloads of children. I was now to be named Nurse First Class Felicia Szwab, daughter of Jan and Emilia, born January 6, 1921 in Kresy Wschodnie, Galicia. Nationality: Polish. Religion: Roman Catholic.

On our trucks were two nuns, a priest, two Polish police-men, and an elderly German guard. We travelled all day, stopping for food, inspections, and for the children to use the toilets, as well as for gasoline and water. I saw Jews working on the roads, guarded by civilians and soldiers. I avoided their gaze; I had to overcome an irrepressible impulse to speak to them, to look into their eyes, for I felt that I had betrayed them.

Late at night we reached a village in a mountainous section in the Cracovian District. Our trucks parked in the yard of an old klasztor, *the Church of the Holy Virgin. The children were sleeping, and we carried the little ones in our arms into an old building in back of the church.*

The Reverend Mother greeted me warmly, and asked about the health of the children. She complimented me on my Polish, and wished me a good night's rest. "May the Lord watch over you."

This klasztor *(church), the nuns, and the children were
my home and family until the end of the war. They gave us
books to read about the Virgin Mary, about Jesus, about the
history of Poland, but they never tried to convert us. However, the children and I did attend Mass, and some of the
children with health problems or distinctive Jewish features
were given up for adoption to Polish families and were bap-
tized.*

*From time to time, German officers came to Mass or to
a program presented by the children. They brought gifts and
left food packages at the door of the orphanage. When the
area was liberated by the Russians, a number of Jewish officers serving in the Polish and Soviet armies established special
guards around our church and orphanage to protect the nuns,
nurses, and female personnel from drunken soldiers and travelling refugees on their way home from slave labor in Germany.*

*Some of the children were returned to the Jewish
Children's Home in Helenowek, Lodz. I stayed with the remaining 22 children until the end of the war. Some of the
newly arrived children were orphans, suffering from TB, tra-
choma, and other diseases. The Swedish Red Cross extended
an offer to take them into their sanitariums. The Jewish Labor Committee in New York planned to open a children's
home in Paris.*

*I wrote to David Dubinsky in New York, offering my
services. I said goodbye to the Sisters of Mercy. We hugged and
we cried. We prayed together for peace, for a free Poland
without religious persecutions, without hatred toward people
of another race or religion. I was raised without religion, but
this time I prayed sincerely, with all my heart. "God, if there*

is a God, please help us overcome the rejection and hatred with which we are surrounded. Bring peace to this country, to all its people and protect the well being and health of these Sisters of Mercy, the nuns and workers here, who risked their lives to save these children and me.

This, dear Sholom, completes my story. It answers your questions about my life during that period. What I really lived through is hard to express in words. More about my life in Paris, and how I met Oscar, I will tell you some other time. Our task now is to reach our goal, to make good on our promise to build the apartment building this year. I might add that Oscar is encouraging me to work with you on this important project, and has promised to help in any way he can.

P.S. Enclosed you will find some pages from my diary.

7

THE LIFE OF A NUN is a daily struggle to conquer frailties, a willingness to follow orders day by day, and to educate yourself to the glory of God. Behavior, manners, prayer, and charitable deeds are part of daily life, just as are the jobs of cooking, cleaning, teaching, and healing.

Since the war began I have had sleepless nights. I pray a lot to tame my fears, not for myself, but for the children. I go to sleep with God on my mind, and wake up with God on my lips, "Lord, Jesus Christ, save the children."

So Sister Zoshia spoke to me last night. She had found me in the chapel past midnight, crying. "You must not cry," she whispered, "you must learn how to pray."

No one had ever spoken to me like that. I listened in silence to her simple words: "With Mother Superior, there are no days of relaxation. Only hard work, obedience, denial of self, living only for Christ and doing His work by saving these children. We must master the intricacies of rationing, and fulfill all orders for the German Hospital and the defense shops. We live here in self-exile, away from a road, but it is lucky for us that we are totally isolated. Our habit saves us and saves the children. But for how long? Only God knows. Christ teaches us to love one another. I came here, not under orders, but of my own choice. So did you. We all go through hours of depression, and moments of nostalgia. You wonder what happened to your parents. I wonder what happened to my brother. Go back to your cell. Soon the children will be awake. They need us, they need you."

We were ordered to make hospital garments, cotton coats, for the Cracow Military Hospital, so the Germans delivered six sewing machines. On one of the machines, in Yiddish, someone had engraved, 'Leah loves Shmuel.'

We do not get paid for our work, but the Germans deliver a weekly ration of potatoes and sugar beets to the convent. The Polish woman who taught us how to sew picks up the completed piles of coats every other day. She told us that all Jews in the small towns around us were being relocated to Malkinia (Treblinka), to Wlodawa country (Sobibor), and Eastern Malopolska (Belzec). The Jews of Cracow were expelled to a camp nearby called Oswiecim and were executed there. Many members of the Polish underground had also been taken to this camp. No longer was it a secret that all the Jews were doomed.

She left us a newspaper called "Barykada" in which was written:

> "The liquidation of the Jews on Polish soil is of great significance for our future development, since it will free us from several million parasites. The Germans have greatly aided us in this matter."

I'm angry and hurt. I don't care what will happen to me, but I'm saving this newspaper, along with my notes in the convent.

I can't understand how, in a time of war, terror, grief, anguish, and days and nights full of fear, I am able to sit

*down with the children and read stories to them. Today I was
reading a magical story by Janusz Korczak, "King Matius the
First." The children listened attentively, but when I finished,
they did not ask questions about the characters in the story,
but about the author.*

*I told them that Janusz Korczak was a Jewish doctor,
and that his real name was Henryk Goldszmidt and that he
was the founder of several orphanages in Warsaw. I can only
imagine what has happened since then. I don't even know if
he is still alive.*

*When I finished, a child asked, "If he is such a good
man, will God let him die?"*

*Lately the children are asking a lot of questions about
God: What does He look like? Is He really sitting on a throne,
surrounded by angels? Why is He so angry with us, His children? I wish I had answers to their questions.*

*My biggest headaches are the nights. The children cry,
talk in their sleep, call "Mamashi" in Yiddish. Sometimes
they forget their fictitious Christian names and call each other
Sarale or Yankele. Some of the older children ask when* Yom
Kippur *(the Day of Atonement) is.*

*I overslept this morning. I was up after midnight with
one of the children who was screaming, "Don't take my father!" I ached for that child, for all the children. I was awak-
ened from a nightmare and jumped up when I felt Sister
Zoshia gently touch my shoulder.*

*Felicia, get up! Are you crying again? Sit up and talk to
me."*

*Everything is wrong. I am out of place here, the
children's faces turned yellowish, they look sick, I can't help
them.*

I started to cry again.

Sister Zoshia touched my face, with her fingers she gently wiped off the tears.

I am working with children in many capacities for the last eight years. I never worked with Jewish children. I can understand their feelings, their pain, the bitterness and grudges. I know how hard it is for you and the children to pretend to be something they are not. I know we need better food than just kapusta *(cabbage) and potatoes, but we live in a war situation, surrounded by enemies. We live in a time of misery, horror, and anguish. There is suffering, grief, and torment all around us. I pray with all my heart for strength, not for my own safety, but for energy enough to sustain and save the children. When I read what is going on in our country, the hate that is directed at us, I also cry. But feeling sorry for ourselves or for our people will not save one child. When you hear them scream, embrace and comfort them. Wipe away their tears. Is that too much to ask?*

"You know that we are under tight controls by the Germans, whose goal is to destroy our church and enslave our people. They began with the Jews and now they are murdering Poles and burning towns and villages all over the Soviet Union. Their armies are proceeding unabated all over Europe and Africa. Their slogan is: "Today Europe; tomorrow the world." The only resistance we can give is to try to survive, to save any man, woman, or child who seeks our help. Our answer to their cruelty is compassion and love. Their day of judgement will come. Until then, we must live, pray and act accordingly. You are a nurse. In the Bible, in the Book of Exodus, there were two Hebrew nurses, Shiphrah and Puah, who chose to ignore Pharaoh's command to kill all newborn Hebrew male children. They obeyed the inner voice of compassion and saved the children. Among them was the child Moses. . . . Who knows? Maybe there is a Moses among the

children we care for in our Klasztor?

"Get up, Felicia. The children need you; they need us. We are essential to their survival."

She smiled, holding back her own tears and turned back to the door.

The Children — I am constantly hammering home a point to them: Do not speak Yiddish among yourselves because sometimes one child gets angry at another child and dangerously curses at him in Yiddish — "Do not cry; only sissies cry."

When a child asks me if he will ever see his Mommy again, I must be strong when faced with that type of question. I cry myself to sleep each night, thinking about my own parents.

Today I was asked to train the older children to do some supporting jobs in our sewing shop. The Germans are demanding the delivery of more and more hospital coats. Mother Superior justifies her request to use the children in the shop by saying it is good for the welfare and security of the children, and the Germans are pleased with our convent's cooperation and help. Civilians continue to pick up and deliver the coats twice weekly, and the Germans consider us law-abiding citizens.

Sister Zoshia tells us that we must increase the output of coats. "I don't want the Germans to come for a visit. We don't want their attention.

I am hungry, but I can't figure out for what. It's surely not for food. I think it is more a mental starvation. With my experiences in Smorodna and Lodz, I lost my appetite, along with my belief in all moral or spiritual nutrition. I feel mocked by idealists who used phrases like "social justice," and "brotherhood." When the evil of fascism invaded Poland, the idealists helped us with their merciless silence. All the ideals and slogans I was raised on and fed with surrendered to pessimism. They became a travesty of words, and dried up.

The "isms" became a caricature for the ludicrous treatment we received from the Nazis, while our idealistic neighbors looked on passively.

The only thing that gives purpose and strength to my life, the only spark of light, is the kindheartedness of Sister Zoshia. In situations when our lives are threatened on a daily basis, she is never angry, always calm. She never screams at the children, and on the occasions when they misbehave, she simply says "these children have been punished enough already."

When the children try their best to make me angry, and I am tempted to punish them, I just stop. But Sister Zoshia sees the world from a different and unique perspective — Mary and Jesus. I don't believe in the Father, so how can I believe in His son? The only thing I am devoted to is the rescue of the children.

The children respect and admire Sister Zoshia. What motivates her — is it pity, compassion, religious zeal? I can't figure it out. Why is she doing all this for us?

Recently, Sister Zoshia gave me a booklet to read, a Reference Book for Nurses that comes from Philadelphia and was published by Lippincott Company in the United States of America. While learning diagrams of pressure points showing the relation of arteries and bones, and learning about contagious diseases, rashes, pox, and other maladies, I learned how to read, spell, and write English. Sister Zoshia found this booklet in the Klasztor Library. I only wish I had the strength, patience, and time to really study, none of which is to spare here.

Today, two German women doctors came to our Klasztor (convent). I offered to show them around, but they declined. As I stood at the door, they approached the statue of the Madonna and the crucifix. Not aware that I was watching, they knelt, buried their faces in their hands and crossed themselves. On their way out, they threw coins and paper money into the wooden alms box.

They wanted to see the children's ward, but Mother Superior advised against it. "We have several children who are ill, and regulations forbid any visitors." Mother Superior, speaking in perfect German, offered the women tea, while Sister Zoshia paraded the children, in groups of ten, from the courtyard to the chapel for prayers. Wearing my nurse's habit and clattering sandals, I joined the two doctors standing at the door of the chapel, listening to the children chanting Ave's, while the jeep driver drank his tea and spoke in Polish with Sister Zoshia.

After they left, Sister Zoshia told me that the driver made a wisecrack, meant to be a compliment. He had said, "With a nice face and figure like hers, I wouldn't mind taking her out dancing."

"Because of you I became a liar. I told him that you were a nurse who will become a nun any day now."

The female in me was flattered. The Jewess in me was afraid for my life. I hope he never comes again.

What I write is more for myself than for any future reader. I live in a dizzying time when things change every day. The world around me is silent, while Nazi thugs murder innocent people. Yet no one says anything. In school, I was told that silence is a fence for wisdom. "If speech is silver, silence is gold." I don't accept this. I don't know if we will survive, but I want to leave my thoughts in writing.

*Sister Zoshia is a strong fighter, confronting a bewilder-
ing array of problems. I am envious of her strong faith. I ask
myself, "What is my goal here? What is my purpose of living?"
It doesn't make sense to want to survive, when the same
people who help the children are preaching that their parents
deserve to be killed or exiled after the war ends. Even in the
underground newspaper they write, "First we will kill the
German Fascists, then we will get rid of the Jews." Why go on
living? It doesn't make sense.*

*When I was still in school, I remember a student asking
our teacher why the Diaspora was lasting so long. Our
teacher answered, "It is because God is so far away." My
teacher believed in the oneness of all humanity; that all be-
ings are a part of this universe. He believed that through
unity and progress, we can overcome all the complexities of
our world, and we will reach liberation and peace.*

*The war defused my teacher's ideals. Pain and fear are
now ruling our world. My only aspiration is to avoid being
dragged down into this pit of darkness we all face. My mind
is overwhelmed with fear and discouragement. Every night I
cry in anguish. Every day immense fear grips my soul. I feel
so small and so lost, and I have no strength left in my heart. I
desperately need a spark of courage, one touch of faith, of
love, of hope, that the children here in this* Klasztor *will one
day see a glimpse of freedom, that one day we will walk out
of here, away from living a lie to reclaim our true names.*

◆ ◆ ◆

*The woman who delivers the bundles of material for our
sewing room also brought us cakes of soap bearing the initials*

R.J.F. — Rein Judishes Fett. This soap, she said, is produced
in Brzezinka-Birkenau Lager, from human fat. The people
know what kind of soap they are using, but they buy it any-
way, using their ration coupons, because there is no other soap
available.

◆ ◆ ◆

Merciful God. . . .
A manifold of pangs, myriads of complaints
are nestled in the hearts of the children,
there is nothing that can dispel the sadness
of missing parents, lost relatives.

Some of them are praying every night
in Yiddish, Hebrew and Polish, lifting
their little hands: Oy, Merciful God!
Please save my Mamashi and Tatashi . . .

There is no response to their quiet pleas,
they feel forsaken like little outcasts,
shut off from the world around them,
robbed of their names, parental love.

They live here in isolation, steady fear,
surrounded by nuns, feeding, teaching, caring,
but detached from them by their own anxiety;
afraid to be discovered by the vicious enemies.

There is no one to give them hope,
they weep at night and I cry with them.
We crave for His compassion and help.
There is no response from the Merciful God. . . .

8

January, 1945.

The Germans are chasing prisoners of Auschwitz through our village toward Germany. Escorted by SS men, they can hardly walk, and many drop from exhaustion. Those who couldn't endure the rigors of the march were beaten or killed. We are allowed to give them water and some bread, but we are not allowed to talk to them. Some prisoners escaped and are hiding in our convent and in the surrounding forest. Some were taken in by local people.

Today, the Russians and units of the Polish army arrived. A Jewish medic from Lodz asked me if we could spare some nurses to go to Auschwitz to help care for some children who survived. They were sick as a result of the medical experiments done on them by the Nazis. The Jewish medic told us that the survivors were suffering because theyr were eating too much food given to them by the liberators. There were about 5,000 people still alive, who are sick, starving, dazed, simply bones held together by skin.

Sister Zoshia, two other nuns, and I took medications and left immediately with the medic. There was talk about rapes and thefts by drunken soldiers, looting at the camps by poor Poles, carrying off clothes, shoes, and valuables left in the warehouses.

We decided to stay for the day and help, not only the children, but the prisoners.

We heard stories about resistance, and the last executions in Auschwitz. Four Jewish girls, Roza Rebata, Ala Gertner, Regina Safirztain, and Esther Wajcblum, had been charged with organizing and supplying the powder used for the explosives that destroyed Crematorium IX last year. For their participation in the revolt, the girls were hanged on the fifth of this month.

In Birkenau, we found corpses stacked up like fire wood. The survivors kept telling us of systematic, day-by-day beatings, starvation, torturing, mass murder in the gas chambers, hangings, and shootings. Many survivors were unable to talk, and could neither stand nor walk. With the permission of the Russians, we helped them exchange their camp uniforms for clothes from the warehouse and were sent to hospitals in Cracow, Katowice, Walbrzych, and other places. The children who were able to walk and could function on their own were taken to our Children's Home and are now being cared for there.

With the permission of the Soviet Commandantura *and the help of the newly established* Zydowski Komitet *(Jewish Council) in Cracow, and with money and provisions from the American Joint Distribution Committee, we are leaving for Paris, France.*

The Russians are anxious for us to leave the area because they are worried about our safety. Their leaders are atheists when it comes to religion, but they are uneasy about having young nuns and nurses in their area when hordes of drunken soldiers are looking for women.

I was thinking of leaving the Home and going to Smorodna to search for survivors, and then leaving Europe. I'm thinking of severing all ties with my past, but I love and

*respect Sister Zoshia, and she insists that I take the children
to Paris. She told me, "Neither baptism, conversion, rejection
of Judaism, nor shedding your religion, will change you. You
survived, and you will remain Jewish. The Lord protected you
and you survived because you helped these children in the
shadow of death. The war is not yet ended, and these children
still need you. Go with them with the Lord's blessing. I will
always pray for you."*

◆ ◆ ◆

*I was shocked and stunned to see a military truck with
two Russian officers and a civilian Pole wearing a red arm
band emblazoned with a hammer and sickle rumble up to
the* Klasztor *gate and approach Mother Superior's room. A
few minutes later, the officers came down the stairs, with
Mother Superior in tow.*

*With her long, thin hand she made the sign of the cross
and quietly said "Dowidzenia (goodbye). May God grant you
perseverance."*

*Sister Zoshia, startled by the swiftness of their departure,
asked the Polish civilian what had happened. "Your Mother
Superior is German. She comes from a family of Nazi collaborators. Her brother was a scoundrel and an informer, and
your Mother Superior used the convent to work for the occupiers, mending uniforms, and producing hospital robes for the
German military."*

*They closed the door behind her and sped away. We har-
nessed our horse and buggy, and Sister Zoshia, four of the
Jewish children, and I rushed to the Military*
Commandantura. *A guard stopped us, and told us to wait.
The truck with Mother Superior inside, was still parked at*

the entrance to the one-story building. A Polish civilian came out asking what we wanted.

Sister Zoshia, her voice trembling and her hands shaking, told him, "Mother Superior risked her life to save twenty-eight Jewish children and two Jewish women. Here are four of those children and one of the women she saved."

"Our informant told us that your Mother Superior had an affair with a German in Cracow."

"God forgive you for saying this. The only affair Mother Superior had is with Jesus Christ. We can verify that she was thoroughly unpleasant to visiting Nazi functionaries. Yes, we sewed hospital robes, but it was just to keep our cover in order to protect the children."

The civilian told us to wait. He came back with a Russian officer who asked the four children to follow him. Two of the girls were reluctant to leave us. They were afraid because they had heard that drunken soldiers had molested children in the nearby village, but the officer spoke to the children in Yiddish, "Hot nit kein moyre (don't be afraid)."

Sister Zoshia nodded to the children to follow the officer. We waited for a long half-hour. Finally, the door swung open and the children came out. We didn't have time to ask them any questions, for immediately we were asked to follow the civilian inside. At a long desk sat an earnest looking officer and a young woman in a military uniform. They offered us chairs to sit in and water to drink.

Then the woman shot questions at us. What were our names, places of birth, parents' names, and occupations before the war, and where were they now? They already knew the names of all the children, the nuns, and the civilian help in the Klasztor (convent). The woman seemed to just make marks next to the names, verifying our statements.

*The officer asked if we'd ever seen Mother Superior leav-
ing the convent in a German military vehicle. "Never! she
was German through and through, but she was anti-Nazi.
She loved God in a thousand ways, and she loved the children."*

*"Just answer the questions without additional com-
ments."*

*Suddenly, the Jewish officer turned to me, speaking in
Yiddish, "I see you lived on Christian documents here. Who
provided these documents?"*

"Mother Superior, through Sister Zoshia."

"Did you convert to Christianity?"

*"I did not. I don't believe in their God or in the Jewish
God. Where were they when the Nazi murderers and their
accomplices killed our people?" I started to cry, and for the
first time in years, since I'd left school, I felt a man's hand on
my shoulder and on my face.*

*"Please calm down. I feel the same. I lost all my family
in Berditchev and in Babi Yar." I looked at his face and saw
tears falling on the medals on his chest.*

*"This woman you've arrested deserves a medal for her
heroism. She was a genius in protecting and hiding these
Jewish children and, believe me, it was not an easy task. We
survived thanks to Mother Superior and to Sister Zoshia, next
to me. I am willing to take her place as a guarantee that she
will not try to escape. Please, let her go back to the Klasztor
to help with the evacuation of these children to Paris and to
Sweden, and the other orphans to Lodz."*

*"That won't be necessary. If you and Sister Zoshia will
just sign a swiadectwo (document), you will be free to take
her with you." An hour later, after signing four long sheets of
yellow, hand-written papers in Russian and Polish, we were*

all on the road back to the Klasztor.

"*Were you scared?*" *Sister Zoshia asked.*

"*No, the Lord was with me,*" *replied Mother Superior.*

That evening, while getting myself and the children packed for the trip to Paris, there was a soft rapping at the dormitory door, and Mother Superior came in. "*I came to thank you, and to wish you a safe journey.*"

"*I want to thank you for saving our lives, my life. Please, have a seat.*"

"*No, thank you. I've got too much to do. We also have to leave this place in the next forty-eight hours. I heard that you cried, begging for my release. I'll always remember you in my prayers. Goodbye, Felicia.* Dowidzenia. *Return to your people and find God.*"

She walked towards the door, turned, and came back, and took me in her arms. She kissed my forehead and said, "*I'm German, you know. I ask your forgiveness for what my people did to you and others in this war. No power will ever erase the crimes committed by the Nazis on the Jews, on humanity, and on our country.*"

That was the last time I saw Mother Superior. When our trucks left the next morning I saw her shadow behind the curtain of her window, watching us leave, her hand making the sign of the cross.

◆ ◆ ◆

For five years I have been sequestered from my world. It isn't a jail, but an isolation from my people, my culture, and my language. My name and my whole existence have been anonymous. I've been watched by men and women, soldiers and nuns, like people look at an object of art, something to be bought, used, and discarded. My whole existence during this time has been a myth, an illusion.

Life feels meaningless. I've never known what true love is; I've only lived for the children. I lead the children to prayers, but it is so trivial and degrading, such a contradiction. Their parents were killed by the Nazis, by Lutherans and Catholics, yet German officers come to our chapel Mass. And here, a group of nuns, Sisters of Mercy, risk their lives to save these children.

Paradoxically, I am filled with jealousy for the woman who deserves my gratitude, Sister Zoshia. I am so frivolous and she is so serious. My heart is full of hostility and hate for the oppressors, the occupiers, the murderers of innocent people, and she is full of compassion, of love for the children, and pity for the enemy.

For every question she has an answer, quoting the Gospel. I feel like an empty shell, archaic and primitive, listening to Sister Zoshia recite quotations from the Old and New Testaments. "Everything that happens is the will of our Lord. As it is written: the Lord has made everything for his own purpose."

I am now on my way to Paris, to freedom, to my own people, my own language and culture. The children will be cared for in a Jewish sanatorium, but what about my life, my self? What are my desires, my dreams? Are they about true love? Having lived for five years under a false name, craving my freedom and my enemy's destruction, having lost my family, my home, my ideals about a better world, where do I go? I feel excluded from humanity, from life itself. The traumas of the last five years need a release. I want to be released from the past.

I am thinking of Sister Zoshia's ideals of universal com-

passion. I want to rid my mind of the rage and grief, suspicion and hostility of the past five years, and find a man who will love me, laugh with me, and share my dreams. And I need God, something to believe in, to trust in, to pray to. I need something that will bring me back to my people, part of the remnants of the Holocaust.

I want to rid myself of the shadows on my face. Reading what I just wrote, I think it's madness.

(On the way to Paris.)

9

*FINALLY, FINALLY WE ARRIVED IN PARIS! Actually, this is not
a regular children's home, but a sanatorium located in a little
town called Bruno, about twenty kilometers outside Paris.
The sanatorium consists of six buildings in the midst of a
magnificent park.*

*"The sanatorium is designed for children who are recov-
ering from illnesses and who are still suffering from the results
of the privations they endured under the Nazis." This is how
it was described on the questionnaire we had to complete
when we arrived. "We need not only your know-how, but
your love for these children."*

*"Their parents were shot, deported, or are otherwise un-
able to care for them. They lived through the grueling years of
the war, concealing their Jewish identity. Now you will call
them by their Jewish names, sing with them Yiddish songs,
and recite Yiddish poems. You will be their teachers, nurses,
mothers, and older sisters, their family. This Vladeck sanatorium will serve as a model, both for educational and medical
institutions."*

*The first thing I did when we arrived was march the
children to take a bath and give them new clothes. Some of
them were still wearing their Christian medallions and were*

reluctant to take them off. "You're sure the Nazis are not coming back?" a little girl asked.

By the next morning, rested, washed, and fed, they were playing hide-and-seek in the sanatorium yard, running in circles and laughing. Oh, when was the last time I heard our children laughing?

The only one who kept to himself was Jacek, little Jacob. He didn't even smile. He was the first one to give up the little cross he was wearing. "I'm not afraid anymore. I'm going to learn Yiddish and Hebrew so I can pray like my father used to pray," he said to a visiting emissary of the American Jewish Labor Committee, Mr. Nathan Chanin, who was moved by the warm reception our newly arrived children from Poland gave him.

I gave Mr. Chanin a letter for my father's friend, David Dubinsky, thanking him for his help in transferring our children from Poland to the B. Charney Vladeck Home in Paris.

I am free! I am myself again. I've gotten my name back. Goodbye Klasztor, your place warmed and saved my body while my soul was angry and hurt.

I scrubbed, cared gently for children who were crying through the nights, uttering sounds in Yiddish — Mameshi! During daytime, their faces showed no expression.

Now, the nights are so peaceful here, but still the children cry, calling Mama! Desolation is a wound that does not heal, not for these children, and not for me.

But, I am free! I am myself again. But I can't erase, scrape off, the past. The inferno of my scorched hometown still smoulders, burning in my memory.

♦ ♦ ♦

I feel good to be with the children at this Vladeck Preventorium. It's like being with family. Not as freilach (happy) as it was at the Helenowek Home in Lodz before the war, but better than in the constantly frightening atmosphere of the Klasztor. The children came here undernourished, sick, and afraid, and lonesome for their parents. They were saved by good people, and hidden among strangers who could not show affection for them.

Here we have loving surroundings, good food and medical care, caring teachers, and love letters from "parents" in America who "adopted" children through the Jewish Labor Committee, Workmen's Circle branches, and the trade unions.

The letters are from people in New York, written in Yiddish, with many English words in them. There are also English letters from Christian members of trade unions, very heart-rending, sentimental, and sweet, like the packages with gifts they send to "their" children. They send gifts such as fountain pens, school bags, and sweets. It makes me feel good to see how the weak, physically underdeveloped children gain weight and, with every passing day, are made well again.

Thanks to Bertha Mering, the Jewish Labor Committee's representative here, we received a load of packages from New York. They send foods which are not available here.

There is still a shortage of some food items and of medicines like Aureomycin and Streptomycin. We need these medications for a group of children who arrived from Poland suffering from TB. Children are still coming here because Poland is in the grip of rampant anti-Semitism.

Last night I heard Charlotte, one of our young girls, telling us how the Germans came to the house when she and two other children were sick in bed with measles. The Germans took her father, and she never saw or heard from him again. Her grandparents were also taken away and deported to a concentration camp. *Charlotte, her mother, and her sisters escaped, but suffered many hardships in hiding and, as a result, are all susceptible to TB.*

Her mother is confined to her home with an active case, and Charlotte and her twin sister live here in the Vladeck Home, in a special pavillion where they are receiving care and medical treatment.

When I heard her talk about how the French fascists helped the Gestapo seize her father and grandparents, I was disgusted and ready to leave France, but where would I go? Palestine? The English are sending many Holocaust survivors to Cypriot detention camps and then back to Germany.

I have written to David Dubinsky and Benjamin Tabachinsky, but so far have not received an answer. They are looking for nurses for Mama Irma's Orphan Home at Erba Como, near Milan, Italy. Who knows if Italy is better than Poland or France?

10

OVER THE LAST THREE MONTHS, Sholom had been out almost every night at meetings, face-to-face solicitations, and fund raising parties. The meeting last night wasn't over until past midnight because they were debating the travel plans to Poland and Israel with a representative of *Histadrut* Tours.

When Sholom got home, Bettsie was watching television in bed. He prepared for bed, but when he tried to cuddle up to his wife she pulled away from him. "How much longer will you be entangled with this project?" she asked.

"It's almost over. We're going to Israel and Poland for the dedication of our building. After that, we will have a community dinner, and then the campaign will be finished. Would you please, please join us on the mission to Poland?"

"No I will not. I'm just not interested. I feel strange among your compatriots. They always speak Yiddish. Frankly, I'd rather stay home with the children. You don't need me there anyway. Every time I've asked you to go out with me or with my friends for dinner you have another excuse, another meeting."

"I'd like to finish this project. It really means a lot to me."

"Your project and your *landsleit* are more important to you than your family."

"That's not true. I love you, Bettsie. You and the children." Again he reached for her hand, and again she pulled away.

◆ ◆ ◆

Sholom decided to come home for lunch. He and Bettsie ate, talked about the children's plans for the summer, and then he asked her to go to bed with him.

"No, I'm playing tennis this afternoon. Why all of a sudden?"

"I will miss you. I'm going away this weekend for three weeks."

"Come home early tonight."

"I can't. We're having a meeting about our final travel arrangements."

"Will Frumele be at this meeting, too?"

"Yes."

"Go sleep with her."

"She is happily married, and so am I."

"You call this happiness?"

Sholom stretched out his hand across the table to her. "Bettsie, don't talk foolishly. You and our children are all I care about. Frumele is my friend, my *landsfrau*. She is as devoted to Oscar as I am devoted to you and the children.

"This project is very important to me, to Frumele, and all our landsleit. Please, you can still join us on this mission. If you feel better at home with the children, stay home, but don't accuse me or Frumele of being unfaithful. Was I negligent? Yes. Disloyal to you? Never!" He tried to put his hand gently on her cheek, but she stood up.

"I'll see you tomorrow morning. I've got to go."

From Frumele's Note Book:

I have no idea who gave Sholom their names.

While we drove on Liberty Road, I discovered their names on our list of landsmen.

We stopped at the shopping center and telephoned the people we wanted to visit.

A woman answered the phone.

Sholom told her that we are Smorodians and are collecting funds for surviving landsleit. We are in the neighborhood and would it be o.k. to visit them?

"Who gave you our names?"

"One of your husbands customers, your and our landsman, Paul Kornblitt, a grocer in East Baltimore."

The woman spoke to someone in Polish, then came back to the phone:

"Please come, we read in the newspapers about your campaign".

Sholom parked is car in the driveway of a small cottage.

I rang the door bell and a tall man asked us in.

His name is Alyosha, hers Sandra. (Strange names for landsleit from Smorodna.) On the table in the living room, on the sofa and chairs we saw books and magazines, the walls were naked, not a picture or painting, just around the window there were some cactus plants and flowers.

Sandra must be my age, blue eyes, a subtle face, but her hair is gray. Alyosha is tall and skinny, looks like a seaman, brown skinned, tense and jittery, strangely quiet.

He sat opposite Sholom, who explained in details the nature of our visit.

"Felicia and I are both survivors. I was in Treblinka, Felicia was in hiding in a Klasztor, we both lost our families. There are some survivors who came back from Siberia and from the partisans, they need our help."

They listened in silence, leaning back in their chairs.

Then Sandra spoke:

"We are descendants from Smorodna but we lived in Lublin. I was in Auschwitz and in Ravensbrook, Alyosha was in the Soviet Union. We came to Baltimore with the help of the Tolstoy Foundation. We lived in the Patterson Park section in East Baltimore and just recently moved to suburbia.

Alyosha is a roofer, repairs and builds deckhouses, he has his own, small shop. It is hard work. Alyosha does everything, siding,gutters,patio enclosures and slate repair. I help him for several hours daily writing estimates, contracts, warranties. . . . I am proud of Alyosha's reputation for excellence in his work.

He works hard and comes home tired, exhausted, all we do is reading books, magazines, we try to catch-up for the lost years. . . . We have no children, no relatives left, we do not belong to any organizations, synagogue or church and we are not interested in our landsmanschaften or lansleit. Alyosha and I read the article in "The Jewish Times" about your Smorodna project, leave us an envelope and we will mail you a donation."

Sholom thanked them for the tea, for listening to us and we walked out to his car.

Sholom was nervous,started the motor but was still

holding on to the steering wheel.

"Strange people, they look frightenly sad."

Sholom was ready to pull out of the driveway when Sandra stopped us:

"Mr. Schwartzman, please wait."

Sandra turned to me and gripped my shoulder:

"Here is an envelope with some cash money for our landsleit. Please, don't list our names as contributors anywhere, no receipts, no thank you letters. . . . This is not a mitzva deed, we do it as an obligation to help our brethren. . . ."

Sholom quietly said to her:

"Thank you and may God bless you."

Sandra almost shrieked:

"God blessed me? Look at my Auschwitz number! Look at my Ravensbroock incision carved on my chest! . . . Alyosha lost his wife and child in Siberia. . . . Damn all God's blessings!"

Sandra pulled her blouse aside showing me a tattoo on her breast. Sholom turned his face away and tried not to look at her. I stepped out of the car and grasped Sandra in my arms.

We just stood there in silence, holding on to each other.

Sholom stopped themotor and we returned to the verandah.

Sandra calmed down, there were no tears left in her eyes but rage, her voice was still nervously vibrating:

"I was in "Block 10" in Auschwitz, the experimental block for stelirization run by Professor Carl Clauberg, Chief physician of the Women's Clinic at the Hedwig Hospital at Kenigsberg. Because of my young age and healthy looks I was chosen to help Dr. Horst Schumann, the assistant to Professor Clauberg and a Jewish doctor by the name of Samuel — I will never forget their names.

One day they hauled us off to houses of prostitution, to a military lager in Placzew, near Crakow. Because of my non-Jewish looks I was consigned to a group of Polish, French and Dutch women. After two weeks a decree came that requested the withdrawal of our group from Placzew and tranfered to Ravensbroock. I was determined to stay with the Polish and Dutch women.

As soon we arrived, we were immediately selected for experiments by Dr. Fritz Fisher. I was given injections and assigned to work. I was working at "Referat B-II" at the SS clothing plant, sorting quilts, featherbeds, blankets, linen and bedsheets for the Volksdeutsche
Mittelstelle (VOMI), the welfare organization for ethnic Germans. I survived the war.

Because of the injections I can't have children. . . .

Alyosha I met at a Displaced Persons Camp in Kassel, Germany. Alyosha was saved and helped by the Russians. . . . We both work hard, try to go on with our lives, but, it is difficult, almost impossible to forget our past. We stay away from people. Our life do not lend itself to conversation. When Alyosha speaks about Russia he continuosly breaks down. . . . We find that whereever we mention a particular episode about our past we are always asked for more details, more questions. It becomes very tiresome and hurting . . .

People ask for explanations that are not easily explainable. . . . Sometimes I can't understand myself from where I get the energy, the stubbornness to go on living. When we arrived in Baltimore we knew no one except the representative of the Tolstoy Foundation. They helped us, invited us to their homes and their church.

We told them that we are disappointed in all religions, that we will support their good work. We continue to help them, we also support the Associated Jewish Charities and other worthwhile causes, but we don't belong to any organizations or groups. . . ."

I promised Sandra that I would call her.

11

THE MISSION TO SMORODNA was a voyage of contradictions. There were feelings of sadness for a lost past and emotional sentiments for the *shtetl* where the compatriots were born and where their parents had lived. They remembered their grandparents walking on the cobblestone streets each morning on the way to prayer; they had recollections of a *Cheder* yard and the synagogue alley full of playful, happy children; they recalled that on Thursdays they had helped their parents carry goods to the marketplace, a tradition that had gone on for centuries.

Smorodna had been the center for mercantile interchange, first between the Russian, and later the Polish military garrison stationed there, and the Jews, residents of this area since the division of Poland in 1740. The Jews were the trading middlemen between the peasants and the officers and their families. Smorodna Jews had called themselves emancipated intellectuals; some were Zionists, some *Bundists,* but most of them, even the so-called intellectuals, were people who gave their children a Jewish education and kept the Jewish holidays. Because of the nature of their trades and businesses, they all spoke fluent Polish.

Hitler killed them all.

When the mission coach arrived in the center of town, none of them, not Sholom, Frumele or the others, recognized Smorodna. The entire town center had been rebuilt by Russian Army units stationed there in the former Polish military barracks. The main street, called Aleje Wolnoscy, was a row of newly erected three-floor apartment units, acquisitioned by the Soviet military for their families.

A new school, Pioneer Center, and a playground had been built where the synagogue once stood.

A young woman tour guide, a representative of Orbis Travel Agency, introduced the group to the mayor of Smorodna, Pan Burmistrz, a polite middle-aged man who spoke in Polish with a heavy Russian accent. Frumele translated his greetings to them and his answers to their questions.

"On behalf of the people of Smorodna, I wish to welcome you to the town of your birth, to the place where you grew up, and which holds for you so many, many memories. I can appreciate how difficult a journey this was for you to make, and if there is anything I can do, please do not hesitate to let me know."

They followed the mayor, listening to him speak: "Our region was made memorable by events of the last war. In 1942 and 1943, the Nazis conducted mass deportations, first the Jewish, and then the Polish population from this region. Over 100,000 people in all were deported.

"Children of this area suffered a terrible fate. Separated from their families, they died like flies during the deportation to the Reich. Some 5,000 Polish children were deported to the Reich for Germanization. Our Smorodna partisans forced the Nazis to stop the deportations. The forest near town was a site of great partisan activities and battles during the occupation. As you travel, you will see monuments on sites commemorating partisan battles southwest of Smorodna."

"Did any Jews return to Smorodna after the war?"

"No, I am sorry to say. When my army unit liberated this town there were no Jews left. They had all been deported to Treblinka. There had been a small group of young men and women who were kept for work by the Germans in their army barracks, but most of them died from disease and starvation. A few escaped to the partisans of Vilna, but the rest were shot by the Nazis on the day they retreated. Only two Jews returned from Siberia after the war. The entire Jewish section was rubble because buildings had collapsed during the Soviet offensive. Those few survivors stayed only a few days in the ruins of their former homes, and then they committed suicide. There had been rumors that two were murdered by vagrants, but the inquiry concluded that they had committed suicide. We found them in the ruins of their homes, their throats cut and a knife between them. In 1946, we razed the remaining buildings and constructed the apartment houses. We built a whole new town.

"How about the Jewish cemetery? It was two hundred years old?"

"The Germans completely eradicated what had been the old Jewish cemetery. They removed all the stones and built barracks for slave laborers and war prisoners right over the graves.

The mass grave at the entrance to our new community park is the only Jewish grave left, and even that the Germans tried to erase. They removed the bodies and used a special machine to crush the bones, and then they burnt the remains and scattered the ashes. When our unit entered the town, we found human bones still lying on the surface. We cleaned up the area and named the place *"Cmentarz Meczennikow,"* the Cemetery of the Martyrs."

The mission people followed the mayor and the Orbis guide for a short stroll on the main street. People watched them, silent and expressionless. They offered no smiles and no greetings.

Frumele turned to the guide, "I think we should leave. I feel the chill in my bones, and I can't take it," but Sholom insisted that they visit the edge of the forest and the new community park.

All the old trees were gone, and new evergreens had been planted. There was a playground and a small soccer field, but there was no sign, no markings on this edge of the *Panstwowy Las* that this was the mass grave of the Smorodna Jews, the ditch that Sholom himself dug for his fellow compatriots, and his own father.

Sholom was painfully aware of the exact location of this place. He dreamed about it constantly. He began to recite *Kaddish,* the prayer for the dead, but broke down before he finished. Frumele cradled him in her arms, and they both wept. The entire mission group cried with them.

From Frumele's Note Book:

My Hometown

> After decades in a distant land,
> I came back to the crumbling home
> of my youth. The ashen house was still
> there and so were the neighbors.

Their cheeks looked wrinkled, ancient,
their faces, like my voice, numb.
All I could think of was a question:
Where were you when all this happened?

They claim not to remember the Germans,
the vanquished city, the arrest of Jews.
I stood there in silence, wondering;
What did you do when all this happened?

Somrodna Park is a grim, desolate place,
I was stirred to tears, thinking that
here perished, vanished my whole family.
Where were You, our everlasting God? . . .

The stillness in the forest, the stray,
black ravens sit on top of the evergreens,
covered by grey dust, did not calm
my deep anger. The loss is too painful.

My hometown changed since I was here,
I myself changed, nerves hardened up.
But, when I think of my dear parents,
I'm still asking: Where were you all?

Did you welcome the Germans with banners?
With bread and salt, with flowers and hugs?
Did anyone show mercy to my relatives
when they were marched to the forest?

My former neighbors look feeble, old,
they claim not to remember anything of

what happened in September-October, 1939.
Today I will leave and never come back . . .

But, Smorodna, the forest, will follow me
for the rest of my life. I will keep asking:
Were you silent bystanders or active helpers?
Whom shall I hold accountable for our loss?

The rest of the mission was as sorrowful as their visit
to Smorodna. In Warsaw, they visited the Jewish Institute
and saw a display of art by Jewish artists who had perished
in the ghetto. They visited the Ringelblum archives, listened to propaganda speeches by government representatives on how well the Warsaw municipality cares for the
remaining eight hundred Jews now living in the city. "We
have a Jewish theater, and we publish a Yiddish newspaper
that serves the 5,000 Jews still living in Poland."

They visited the Gensza Jewish cemetery where Pinchas
Shainitz, the custodian, a man in his sixties, guided them to
the grave of Mordecai Anilewicz, the commander of the
Warsaw Ghetto uprising. They also went to the Nozik *Shul,*
the only remaining synagogue in all of Warsaw. It had not
been destroyed because the Nazis used it as a stable for their
horses. On the way from the synagogue they were surrounded by elderly Holocaust survivors who thanked the
group for coming to Poland, saying, "Please, don't forget
us!"

They stopped at the former *Umschlagplatz,* the embar-
kation point where Jews from the ghetto were rounded up
and marched to the railroad station and into the cattle
trains to Treblinka. A plaque, written in several languages,
informed visitors that from this place hundreds of thou-

sands of Jews were taken to be executed in the concentration camps.

The group walked to the monument at the site of Mila 18, and then to the Monument to the Heroes and Martyrs of the Warsaw Ghetto Uprising. They placed flowers and a wreath at the base of the monument and listened to a man reciting *Kaddish.* Then they left for a meeting with the leaders of the Warsaw Jewish community.

While the rest of the Smorodna delegation met with the local Jewish leaders who gave routine answers in the presence of a representative of the communist authorities, Sholom left the meeting, grabbed a taxi, and asked the driver to take him to Piastow. The driver, a man in his mid-fifties, was familiar with the suburbs of Warsaw.

"This city was destroyed, then rebuilt and enlarged." The driver went on to talk about modern Warsaw, its twelve schools, thirty-seven museums and twenty-one theaters.

Sholom interrupted him, "Tell me, please, where were you during the war?"

"I participated in the defense of Warsaw under our mayor, Stefan Starzynski, who was later killed by the Germans. When they began the round up of hostages, in December, 1939, I was taken to a forced labor camp in Germany. I escaped in October, 1944, and returned to Warsaw, only to discover that my wife and four children had been killed during the rebellion in August."

He was quiet for a moment, and then went on. "Life was unbearable after I returned from Germany. Warsaw was nothing but burnt ruins. I got a job in a cooperative, learned how to drive, and decided to stay here. I feel that I belong in Warsaw. The economy is still bad, but how much does one person need? Some of my friends say that I'm crazy,

going back every week to the place where I lived with my
family, where my family was murdered. But I miss them so
much, I can't help but return here."

◆ ◆ ◆

The old houses of Piastow, the streets, the statues, everything, looked remarkably the same. Sholom walked the
three steps to the house where he had lived.

An elderly woman came to the door, "What is it that
you're looking for?"

"Does Pan Jarosz Waclawski live here?"

The woman crossed her hearth, "Jarosz Waclawski died
fifteen years ago. I'm his niece. Who are you?"

"My name was Romanowski. I lived here during the
war. Pan Waclawski was a close friend of my father's. May I
ask you how he died? Was he ill?

"I'm sorry, but I don't know. I only received notice as
the next of kin that my uncle had died. I lived in Old
Brodno in Praga. It was a slum area which the government
decided had to be cleared, so I applied for this house. You
didn't come here to claim this house, did you?"

"No, I just wanted to see the man who saved my life
during the war. After the war, we corresponded and I sent
him money and gift packages, but then suddenly I didn't
hear from him anymore." Still, the woman did not trust
him, and would not invite him into the house. Sholom
went back to his waiting taxi and to the hotel where his
Baltimore *landsmen* were ready to continue their somber
journey to Cracow and Auschwitz.

◆ ◆ ◆

Six hours later they arrived in Cracow. It was raining. The drizzle fogged the windows, and everyone was disheartened. Sholom stood up, took the microphone, and said, "What we saw today was very depressing, but our visit fulfilled a need and a desire to see for the last time the place where we were born. Our very presence here proclaims "We are here! *Mir zenen Do!* The Nazis failed! Our presence attests to the indestructibility of our people. *Am Yisroel Chai!*"

Sholom began to sing, *"Am Yisroel, Am Yisroel Chai!"* Frumele's voice came out of the darkness of the coach. She cried and sang, and the others joined in, *"Am Yisroel, Am Yisroel Chai!"*

In their hotel in Cracow they were met by Matczey Jacubowicz, the leader of the Jewish community of seven hundred survivors. They walked around the old city and visited a synagogue built in the fourteenth century by Jews from Prague. The building, with its beautiful vaulted ceilings, was now a museum. Adjacent to the old Jewish cemetery, they found the Rabbi Moses Isserles *Shul* which was built in 1553 by the Rabbi's wealthy father.

Mr. Jakubowitz pointed out the chandeliers and holy books that had survived.

"Thanks to Rabbi Isserles and his writings, our community gained recognition from kings, philosophers, and scientists," Mr. Jakubowitz proudly explained. "Our community gained immortality when historians wrote of us 'the Holy Community on the Vistula and Volga Rivers.' "

"During the occupation the heirs of Rabbi Isserles, the Jews of Cracow, were herded here in groups of ten, a *"minyan,"* for daily executions. The few of us who returned from the concentration camps, the partisans, and the invalids of

World War II, found everything destroyed. There was nothing left but Rabbi Isserles' tombstone."

They walked around the facade of the tombstone walls to the cemetery where he was buried. Someone said *Kaddish* for the martyrs of Cracow, and offered a donation for the Isserles *Shul.*

Maczej Jakubowitz thanked them for coming. "Don't forget us."

Then they boarded the coach for Auschwitz-Brezinka-Birkenau.

12

FRUMELE KNEW WHAT THIS PLACE WAS. She was there when it was liberated by the Russian and Polish units. She had heard enough about Auschwitz and the other camps from survivors she'd met in Paris and in Baltimore and from articles in newspapers and magazines.

But being here now was most difficult for her. She looked at pictures of children taken for experiments by Dr. Mengele, and pictures of selections, stripped human skeletons, and she shivered. She was thinking of Sandra and Block 10. Walking outside the barracks, surrounded by barbed wire and guard towers, Frumele cried out, "God, where were You?"

The group chanted prayers in Barracks 27, but Frumele felt that prayers here, at Auschwitz, were absurd. She sat outside on the cold ground and the emotions which had been building inside her burst through, and she screamed, "My dear Papa and Mama, why did I survive?"

The visit to Auschwitz profoundly shook Sholom, opening up memories stored in his subconscious, details of his days in Treblinka that he'd never wanted to share with anyone. On the plane to Tel Aviv, sitting next to Frumele, he talked for the first time since liberation. All that Frumele had asked him was what he had done in Treblinka, and

Sholom, as if talking to himself, itemized names and dates, places, and events.

"My job was sorting clothes from the piles of packages lying behind the barracks. The SS men used to pick people from our group, take them to the deep ravine, make them stand on the edge of the abyss and shoot them. This ravine was called the Lazaret and it was used for the sick, the elderly, and the pregnant women who arrived on transports. One day one of those chosen for the Lazaret jumped out and stabbed one of the SS men. He was shot immediately and then the SS guards began shooting into the crowd, pushing people into the ravine with rifle butts and whips. This massacre lasted half an hour. Many bodies were lying around the Lazaret. Lalka, the SS man, assembled our command, randomly chose ten inmates and shot them in front of us, and then he gave a little speech, "*Sie sind under mein herschaft.* Anyone who will try to resist will be shot.""

"Although I said I was a barber, I was still selected to do all kinds of work, cleaning the grounds, sorting valuables, working with the 'dentists,' and carrying the bodies to the pits. I did everything in a hurry, prodded by the whips of the guards. Our own *Kapos* (guards) would chase and beat us. One of the worst *Kapos* was someone named Gustav. He'd hit inmates in the face. If the victim were bleeding or if his face were swollen, Gustav would order him to take his clothes off and jump into the pit; then the SS men would shoot him.

"Once, while I was working as a wood carrier, I was a few seconds late to the *Apel* (line-up) and was punished with twenty lashes on my back. I took it without making a sound, and went back to work carrying wood to burn the dead.

"For a while I worked as a *kartoffelsheiler* (potato peeler) in the kitchen. I was able to eat some raw potatoes in addition to my daily ration. This was my best job in Treblinka.

"In the beginning there were only three gas chambers working, but in September they installed ten new ones. The loading and unloading of the victims took longer than the gassing. The new chambers faced each other; they had narrow windows and the guards were able to look in to see if the victims were dead. Then they opened the gates and threw the corpses out. I was often ordered to join the *Himmelstrasse* Alley to help remove the corpses. I considered suicide, maybe running into the electric fence or hitting Ivan, the Devil, or Micolai, or the operators of the gas-pumping machines. The work was unbearable, but I didn't have the guts to end my life.

"Dr. Irmfried Eberl, the commandant of Treblinka, walked around in his white doctor's coat, writing on a note pad in his hands and talking with the other SS men. When he saw the piles of corpses, he said something to the SS men and they immediately began beating us with their whips, shouting, '*Shneller* (faster)!'

"Beginning in 1943, we had to dig up the dead from the mass graves, and burn them. The stench, flames, and smoke permeated the entire camp. When new transports arrived, the victims were gassed and burned immediately.

"By the summer of 1943, we were put to work planting lupine to cover any traces of the ravines. I thought about escaping while I carried evergreens from the forests, but there were few escapes from Treblinka. One *Kapo* was discovered digging an escape hole. Lalka conducted the line-up and the execution, hanging the *Kapo* upside down and beating, and then shooting, him.

"You know, Frumele, even in Treblinka the Jews didn't lose their faith. We had Jews among us who prayed every night before going to sleep. For some reason, the SS did not forbid prayers. While some prayed, others of us would talk quietly, trying to organize a rebellion and an escape."

"Did you believe in God while you were in Treblinka?"

"I'd ask myself that same question very often. Part of me was thinking of suicide, that there was no God and no justice, but another part of me wanted to live, to survive, to search for my Chanele, and to take revenge. That was my aim, and my hope.

"While I saw my physical energy wearing out — at the same time — I don't know how to define it, but I felt that my fate was manipulated by a higher power. So many times I was close to death and always, at the last minute, some unseen power, some thought, saved me.

"My friend, Rabbi Elimelech Hertzberg, told me that this was God watching over me. In my saddest moments, while waiting for the end, I heard voices calling to me, 'You must survive.' Voices like those told me to help our *landsleit*.

"It is extremely difficult to see what we've seen in Auschwitz, to think of what I endured in Treblinka, to think of our parents and Smorodna, and still believe in God. There were always people, from Elisha Ben Abuyah to Gershon Sholom, who had doubts about God's power. I am not learned enough to understand the ways of God and come to any conclusions. There are so many things that I can't understand. Where were the world's leaders? Where were our Rabbis and other Jewish leaders? I know that I belong to a people, with believers and non-believers. They are my people, the simple ones and the noble ones. The purpose of my living, my going now to Israel, is to help them. If this is God's way of leading me to them, I believe in Him."

◆ ◆ ◆

They arrived in Israel at 3:15 Friday morning. A plane with new immigrants was disembarking at the airport. There was singing and dancing, and no one was tired. The Polish experience was still haunting them, and the songs and the feeling that they were now among their own people was anti-climatic; they were so uplifted, proud and grateful that there was an Israel.

Their first visit was to Ramat Gan. Malka Portugali, Director of Projects for the *Histadrut,* escorted the group to the Chadar Ochel, the restaurant/dining room of Kiryat Siegal. After lunch and speeches by Yehoshua Levy, the treasurer of *Histadrut,* and Nahum Guttman, the editor of the New York magazine *Histadrut Photo News,* the group finally visited their project. The new building was completed and ready for dedication the following Sunday when Ambassador Avraham Harman and his wife, Zena, would return from Washington to be guests of honor at the dedication. They were also waiting for Prime Minister Levi Eshkol to return from his visit to President Johnson's Ranch in Texas.

While in Ramat Gan they also visited Tel Hashomer Hospital and an absorption center.

From Ramat Gan, they travelled to Haifa, stopping on the way at Kupat Holim clinics and a youth *aliyah* center.

After observing the view from the Carmel on the Bay of Haifa, the coach travelled on the Acre (Akko) Naharia

Highway and stopped at the *kibbutz* Lohamei Hagetaot. The Smorodna group visited the Yitzhak Katzenelson Museum, which depicts the pre-war Jewish world of Eastern Europe. The *kibbutz,* in its natural beauty, looks like a health resort, a tourist's paradise. People were visiting the place from all over Israel, among them many Holocaust survivors.

The *kibbutz* was founded in April, 1949, by ghetto-fighters, partisans, and survivors. The Katzenelson Museum is a center of documentation, as well as a memorial honoring the martyrs and heroes. Sholom and Frumele met the co-founder of the *kibbutz* and the museum, Yitzak (Antek) Zuckerman, when he had visited Baltimore.

Dr. Isaac Fein introduced Yitzhak Zuckerman at a special event in the Baltimore Hebrew College as "the ultimate personification of courage, a hero of the Warsaw Ghetto Uprising."

Author Zvi Shner, director of the museum, greeted the Smorodna visitors warmly and introduced them to the stocky figure of Yitzhak Zuckerman. He walked with the group around the museum, showing and explaining with zeal, the exhibit of the tortured children, pictures of Nazi horrors, and the model of the Warsaw Ghetto. Yitzhak and Zvi implored the group to record their life stories.

The manner and warm greetings of Yitzhak and Zvi were fascinating and full of joy. They both wished the group good luck in their undertaking to build a *shikkun* in Kiryat Siegal.

They resumed their travels in an uplifted mood as they continued on to *kibbutz* Gesher Haziv.

13

THE SMORODNA MISSION had hotel reservations in Haifa, about a forty-minute drive from this *kibbutz* in the north-western corner of Israel, just south of the Lebanese border. Instead, they decided to stay out at Gesher Haziv, an agricultural settlement founded in 1949 by a group of Israeli, Canadian, and American youth, many of them from the Baltimore-Washington area, and three of them children of immigrants from Smorodna.

They arrived at the *kibbutz* in the afternoon when most of the people were at work in the fields and gardens. They heard singing and children's voices coming from the nursery and kindergarten, and the beat of hammers from behind the guest house. A man on a tractor greeted them with a hearty, *"Shalom!"*

A young mother and her child were walking in a park and Sholom asked her where he could find Moshe Greenfield of Baltimore. She pointed to a small house surrounded by trees and flowers, with vines covering the porch and windows.

The young woman was Margie Lewis, the daughter of Mr. and Mrs. Milton Cohen of Washington, DC. Her husband, Collin, was at work and she had just picked up their baby, Yair, from the nursery after working a few hours herself. The Baltimore contingent asked Margie about her life on the *kibbutz.*

"I enjoy life here. We are free and happy, and relaxed. The only thing we miss is our parents."

Frumele asked her if she would like to go home for a visit.

"Oh, no, we have a lot of work here. Did you see all the new construction? I want my parents to come here, and the sooner the better."

Mike Duvdevani, one of the founders of the *kibbutz,* greeted the Baltimore delegation warmly and affectionately. He knew most of them, having met them in Baltimore when he'd visited his close friends and co-founders of the *kibbutz,* Malka and Hayim Stopak. Proudly, he showed the delegation the new guest bungalows, the new living quarters for the summer campers, the primary and secondary school buildings, and the Abraham Stopak Cultural Center, built by the Baltimore *Histadrut* Campaign and the family of the late Baltimore Labor-Zionist leader.

"We are busy building more bungalows and playgrounds," Mike Duvdevani explained. "We use the Baltimore Stopak Center for cultural activities and for religious services. We have American counselors who run a summer camp here for our own children as well as new immigrant children. We teach dramatics, arts and crafts, swimming, dancing, Jewish history, sports, conversational Hebrew, and so on. We use all the newest audio-visual equipment."

While Mike was talking, Sholom marveled at the view from Gesher Haziv. From the top of the Abraham Stopak Center, they could see the beaches of the Mediterranean, and, across the way, the ruins of the ancient village of Achziv, mentioned in the books of Joshua and Judges.

"This area belonged to the Tribe of Asher. Now it belongs to the Jewish people, to all of us," Mike remarked. Sholom started to say something, but then stopped. Sy Greenfeld, formerly of Baltimore, turned to Sholom, "Say it in English and I'll translate."

"I just wanted to say that I wish this had belonged to us in 1938 and 1939. I wish we'd had an Israel then. Some of our people would be alive today."

The delegation then followed Moshe Kerem, Mike Duvdevani, and Sy Greenfeld to the guest house for refreshments, good wine, and a photo session. There they were surrounded by more former Baltimoreans who wanted to send messages to their families and friends in the Baltimore-Washington area. "Come visit us! Send us your children!"

Sholom turned to Frumele, "I feel as if I could stay here forever. You know, Frumele, in 1938, my girlfriend, Chanele, wanted to go to Palestine, and my father urged me to join her, but I didn't listen. I did not want to leave him alone, and her parents were reluctant to let their only daughter leave. Now look what has happened."

"This is why we came here, Sholom. We survived, and now we have an obligation to help Israel absorb what is left of European Jewry and Jews from other countries who want to come here." Frumele whispered, "You know, Sholom, I was raised in an anti-Zionist home. My family believed that the future of the Jewish people was in Europe. How I wish my parents had left Europe and gone to Palestine! Maybe they would be alive today."

Sholom helped Frumele carry her small suitcase to the door of her room at the guest bungalow. She turned and gave him a light kiss on the cheek, saying "Thank you, and I'll see you at dinner."

"You are thanking me? For what?"

"For carrying my bag, for being my friend, for bringing me here. See you later. I'm going to take a shower and rest for awhile."

"I think I will, too."

♦ ♦ ♦

Sholom showered, changed into shorts, and laid down on the narrow bed, but he couldn't sleep. His thoughts were of Chanele as he imagined her singing in Hebrew, *"Anu olim Artza"* (We are going to Palestine). "God, what happened to her? To her parents? To our people? Why? Why?"

He finally fell asleep, but another song woke him. It was Frumele, singing in the shower. Sholom got up and opened the door between his room and Frumele's. She was drying her back in front of the mirror, and humming. She looked beautiful.

"Let me help you."

"You scared me!"

"You woke me up."

He embraced her, and for a moment they kissed passionately, but when he led her to her bed, Frumele covered herself with the towel. "Please, Sholom, stop! Please don't. We're both married," she said with exasperation. Her cheeks were burning. "It's not easy for me, either, believe me. But we each belong to someone else."

Sholom stood up. "When I heard you singing . . . please, forgive me. Please don't be angry with me. You know

how much I care about you. Will you take a walk around
the *kibbutz* with me?"

Frumele nodded. Sholom went to the door, turned,
and took her in his arms. She did not resist. "You'll never
know how much you mean to me."

♦ ♦ ♦

Sholom heard someone singing and awoke, grateful
that this was only a dream. He was thinking of Chanele,
dreaming about Frumele, and missing Bettsie. He got up
and tried the door to Frumele's room. The latch was closed.
Quietly, he left his room and walked to the *kibbutz* office
and called home. He let it ring for a long time, but there
was no answer. The children were probably in summer camp,
but where was Bettsie? It was six hours earlier in Baltimore.
Where was she?

♦ ♦ ♦

After leaving Gesher Haziv, the group visited an Amal
Trade School in Zefat, walked around the artist colony of
the ancient city, and then stopped for lunch in Petach Tiqva.
They visited the Dr. Henry Seidel Hospital in Yaffo and the
Ben Ari Museum in Bat Yam. It was supposed to be a quick
visit to the museum, but stretched to two hours of admir-
ing the art and opening up long-hidden memories and emotions when the Smorodner *landsmen* met the curator, Yitzhak
Ginzburg.

14

ABRAHAM ELIEZER GINZBURG was a noted community leader in Lodz, Poland. When the Germans occupied Lodz in September, 1939, he was the owner of a wholesale textile business whose warehouse was appropriated by the Nazis as soon as they invaded the city. He convinced his nineteen-year-old son, Yitzhak, to leave Lodz for Warsaw where they had relatives, and from there to try to crossing the border into the Soviet Union.

Yitzhak bid goodbye to his relatives in Warsaw, and walked until he had crossed the border. He had eluded roadblocks, military posts, and bands of hoodlums waiting on the crossroads for escaping Jews.

A former Yeshiva student, his only work experience had been selling textile materials for his father's business. With no trade, and only a pocketful of worthless Polish money, Yitzhak volunteered for a work battalion and was sent to Pogerzbiczce, where he found work at the local sugar mill.

Several months later, he was mobilized into the Red Army and was sent to the Finnish-Russian border. When the war between Finland and Russia ended, he was demobilized and sent to Balacha, Kazakhstan, to be mobilized again when Germany attacked the Soviet Union in June, 1941. He was wounded at the front at Dniepropetrowsk. When he came out of the Lazaret, he was sent to Karaganda, to Petropawlowsk, and finally to Alma Ata, the capital of Kazakhstan. There he met and married a young officer in the Red Army, Lida Zhukova, and they had a son, Yuri.

Early in 1946, Yitzhak brought Lida and Yuri back to Lodz, to his former neighborhood. They found it to be "a heap of ruins, one large cemetery." Most of the 230,000 Jews of Lodz had perished, including Yitzhak's parents, brother, and sisters. Only 877 inmates of the Lodz Ghetto had survived. They were the group who had been assigned by the Germans to clean up the ghetto after the final deportations.

The terrible reality devastated Yitzhak. Nobody, not one soul from his large family, had survived. Moreover, a virulent, savage, anti-Semitic propaganda was spreading and poisoning the atmosphere all over Poland. The few Jews who returned from the war, some partisans, and a few survivors of concentration camps were physically attacked, and even thrown off moving streetcars.

On July 4, 1946, a *pogrom* erupted in the city of Kielce. Jews were accused of a ritual murder of a nine-year-old boy. A local mob, armed with clubs, axes, sticks and knives, murdered forty-two Jews, and wounded many others.

That week over, 5,000 Jews escaped from Poland to Czechoslovakia. On the way, they were robbed, and some were killed. In the newspapers, Jews were accused of causing all the post-war ills that befell Poland. Despite protests from President Harry Truman and other world leaders, hatred campaigns against the remnants of Polish Jewry continued unabated.

Yitzhak was ready to leave Poland, but he heard that the circumstances in Czechoslovakia, Hungary, Austria, and Germany was not any better than in Poland. In Czechoslovakia, the followers of the Slovak fascist, Hlinka, continued robbing and murdering Jews. In Hungary, Cardinal Mindszenty refused to issue an appeal against anti-Semitic carnage by former Nazi collaborators. In Austria, Jews received threatening letters with sentiments such as, "Hitler's task will be finished only when the last Jews have been liquidated." At a soccer game in Vienna the crowd shouted, "Throw the Jews into the gas chambers!" The Polish press reprinted these news items on the front pages.

Jews attempting to reach Palestine were arrested by the English Navy and sent to concentration camps in Cyprus, Egypt, or back to Germany. Yitzhak decided to stay in Lodz.

Lydia was pregnant with twins, and to travel under such conditions would be life-threatening. Yitzhak volunteered to serve on the Komitet Zydowski (Jewish Council), trying to lessen the pandemonium among the refugees returning from the Russian gulags, from Central Asia, and the mines of Kamchatka.

His committee was also busy placing children who had survived the war in hiding in Christian homes or Church-related institutions, and were being returned to the Komitet Zydowski. The people were afraid that their neighbors would discover that they haad been hiding Jewish children. There were cases reported in the papers that windows had been broken in homes of these Righteous Gentiles, their homes had been set afire, and "Jew-lovers" had been written on their walls. Some of the children, on their own, came to the Komitet looking for their birth parents, hoping that they had survived.

The Jewish Council opened what had been the Helenowek Children's Home, with the financial support of the American Joint Distribution Committee, the Society of Polish Jews, and the Jewish Labor Committee. The religious *Gmina* (Jewish Community Council) provided teachers, and books were sent by Agudas Israel of America and the Vaad Hatzala (Rescue Committee).

Yitzhak divided his time between helping Lida with Yuri and the newborn twins, Bella and Dora, and serving on several important committees on the Council.

◆ ◆ ◆

One morning, while attending a session at Maavak, the organization of former war veterans and former partisans, Yitzhak was told by a secretary that a young woman, a nun, was waiting for him in his office, and that it was urgent.

Yitzhak excused himself and went to his office. "I am Ginzburg, please take a chair."

"I am Sister of Mercy Zoshia."

"What can I do for you?"

"By the grace of the Virgin Mary and her Son, our Lord, we were able to save in our *Klasztor* (convent) the lives of a group of Jewish children. After the war, most of the children were taken by one of our nurses, who was also Jewish and living with us on Christian documents, to Sweden and France.

"When the Russians arrived, the Soviet *Commandantura* requisitioned all of our buildings, and we were transferred to Lodz with twenty-eight children, four of them Jewish. Last week we again received orders to leave our convent, which has been designated by the municipality of Lodz as a

political training school. We've been told that we're moving
to Radom.

"You've lost so many, and so few children have sur-
vived. I feel that these children belong to the Jewish people.
With the permission of our Reverend Mother, and after
prayers to our Saviors and our *Matka Boska* (the Virgin
Mary), we've decided to place the four orphans with you.
Here are their documents, their pictures, and their school
report cards. Here, also, are the documents of Sister Felicia
Szwab; her real name was Fruma, or Frumele Kleinbaum.
She came from a small town called Smorodna. I kept her
papers in our convent library because it was dangerous for
her to have them."

Yitzhak, a man who was far from a believer, listened to
the nun. With tears in his eyes this war-hardened man said
to her, "You are not a nun, but an angel from heaven.
People like you are the hope for the future of mankind."

Looking at the pictures of Frumele with the children,
he said, "This Frumele looks like one of my sisters and you,
dear Sister Zoshia, look like Lida, my wife. May God bless
you with good health. Please forgive my emotionalism. I
promise you that we will take care of the children you so
miraculously saved from the hands of the Nazis. If there is
anything we can do for your orphanage, for the Polish
children, just let me know. I will see to it that the children
will be accepted immediately at the Helenowek Children's
Home.

◆ ◆ ◆

Yitzhak Ginzburg left Poland for Israel in 1957, settling in Tel Aviv. Lida and the children officially converted

to Judaism, and Yuri's name was changed to Yankel. Their apartment was devoid of all elementary comforts, but they were happy to be away from Communist repression, and to be free to send their children to schools of their choice. Yankele showed exceptional talent in art, and was accepted to the Academy of Painting. Bella and Dora excelled in their studies as well, and Yitzhak became curator of the Ben Ari-Bath Yam Museum.

Yitzhak did not forget Sister Zoshia. While still in Poland, he had supported her Home of the Virgin Mary with packages of special foods, medications and clothing for the children that his Komitet received from the Joint-USA. But because of the strict censorship of the Communist regime in Poland, communications with Sister Zoshia ended after the family left for Israel. Yankel, impressed by his father's stories about the Sisters of Mercy and how they saved the Jewish children, used the pictures that Sister Zoshia left with his father as models which he included in some of his early paintings.

One day, a mission of American Jews arrived in Israel, accompanied by survivors of Smorodna living in Israel. They visited the Ben Ari Museum in Bat Yam. The curator, Yitzhak, guided the guests, gave explanations in Hebrew and Yiddish, while Sholom, of Baltimore, translated into English, explanations of the exhibits and the backgrounds of the artists. Of course, Yitzhak was particularly proud to show off his son Yankel's talented works, "Family at Sabbath," "The Dybbuk" and "An Israeli in New York." The people on the mission were fascinated by the paintings of this young artist, and someone remarked, "The painting, 'Madonna of the Poor,' looks like our Frumele. What do you think?" All of the Baltimore delegation agreed.

Sholom went to look for Frumele who was absorbed in a picture by the same Yankel Ginzburg that looked just like Sister Zoshia. "You know, Frumele, we found a painting that looks just like you. Come see."

Yitzhak Ginzburg overheard the name Frumele, turned around, and recognized her.

"You are Felicia? Frumele? I have an envelope with your papers, poems, and notes, given to me by the Sister of Mercy Zoshia in Poland many years ago. I had planned to give these documents to the archives of Yad Vashem in Jerusalem, but I never did. These pictures, painted by my son, are of you and Sister Zoshia."

Yitzhak then invited the stunned members of the mission to his office for refreshments where they listened to Yitzhak and Frumele share the story of Sister Zoshia. "What I am telling you is incomprehensible, but every word I say is truth. It really happened, and I'm so glad that Frumele is here to verify my story.

15

WHILE THE SMORODNA DELEGATION visited the Yad Vashem library and museum and attended the daily memorial service, Frumele walked around the Garden of the Righteous Among the Nations, which commemorates Gentiles who risked their lives to save Jews from the Nazis. She followed a pilgrimage of Christians from many countries, among them foreign dignitaries, nuns, and priests who came to pay their respects to the martyrs of the Holocaust.

Frumele watched a tree-planting ceremony in the Garden of the Righteous, and listened to people speaking Polish, Hebrew, and Yiddish. She heard the voice of Dr. Chaim Pazner, a member of the Yad Vashem Directorate, speaking about "the significance of this ceremony, expressing my heartfelt thanks to this righteous woman, the Sister of Mercy, a nun from Lodz who, with courage and heroism, risked her life to save twenty-three Jewish children in Cracow, Poland."

Frumele impulsively pushed herself forward and shrieked, "Sister Zoshia!" Everyone turned towards the American tourist with no manners, the one who had just disrupted this impressive ceremony.

Sister of Mercy Zoshia turned around and saw Frumele.

"Jesus, Maria, Felicia! My Felicia!"

The two women embraced and cried.

"I'm one of the children she saved," cried Frumele.

After the ceremony some newspeople wanted to inter-view and photograph Frumele and her savior, but they both refused. Holding on to each other, they went to the Yad Vashem cafeteria and shared stories of their lives. Frumele showed her pictures of Oscar, Jacob, and Bernie, her hus-band and sons. Sister Zoshia spoke of her work in a chil-dren's home in Lodz. Frumele asked about her family.

"My parents died after the war. My brother Stefan, the policeman, served in the Polish Army at Westerplatte, the island near Gdansk, under Major Sucharski. He was wounded resisting the German Navy that attacked the is-land with their panzer ship, the *"Schleswig Holstein."* After seven days of resistance, the garrison on Westerplatte sur-rendered, and Stefan, along with the other wounded de-fenders, was taken prisoner. He left Poland with Major Sucharski, served in Italy, and after the war emigrated to America. For a while he lived in Chicago, then he married a girl from Virginia, and now they live near Washington, DC. They have a son who is studying to become a priest, and two daughters. They don't write too often because Po-land is still under censorship."

"My dear Sister Zoshia, please, come visit us. My home will be your home. This is my address. You know, all these years I have wondered why you risked your life to save us, all the children and me."

"The Lord led me to it. Did you ever read in the Old Testament, in Leviticus? It is written, 'Thou shalt not stand by the blood of thy neighbor.'"

"There must have been more to it than just faith."

"There was. I'll make it short. Years before the war, when I was still at school, my family lived in a building shared by many Jewish families. My father took care of building maintenance. One day during a snow storm I fell on the ice and broke my leg. A Jewish boy from our building, Hershko, who was my age and on his way to school, picked me up and carried me on his back for three blocks to the police station where my brother Stefan worked.

"Hershko later went to the Army and I became a nurse, then a nun. When the Germans occupied our city and I saw what they were doing to our Jewish neighbors, I felt that I had to do something, so I decided to save the children. The Lord helped me, Felicia. Here is my address in Lodz. Come visit my children's home on Franciskanska Street."

"Sister Zoshia, there is a man in Tel Aviv, who would like to see you. His name is Yitzhak Ginzburg, from Lodz. He is the curator of a museum in Bat Yam."

"Holy Mary! Pan Ginzburg lives here? I lost contact with him. You know, the Communist system is very cruel to people who had contacts in foreign countries, especially with Israel. Please, let me have his address and telephone number."

They hugged and cried again. "May the Lord watch over you, Felicia."

"I wish you only good luck and good health."

Sister Zoshia returned to her entourage and Frumele went back to her coach which was ready to leave for Ein Gedi in the southern part of Israel.

Everyone on the coach was talking about the visit to the museum and the memorial ceremony, and some were taking pictures of the Negev, its peaks and canyons. Frumele leaned on Sholom's shoulder, closed her eyes, and thought about Sister Zoshia, the children in the Vladeck Home in Paris, her own children, and Oscar.

"Where were you?" Sholom asked. "I was looking all over for you?"

"I happened upon my savior during the war."

"You've become a believer?"

"I've begun to believe in human goodness. I was with the nun who saved my life."

Frumele shared with Sholom her unexpected meeting with Sister Zoshia at The Garden of the Righteous Among the Nations.

For an entire week the group travelled all over Israel. They met with government and *Histadrut* leaders, visited the *Arava kibbutzim* and the salt plains of Sodom, ate lunch at an army post with Israeli soldiers in the Jordan valley, and took pictures with Teddy Kolleck, the Mayor of Jerusalem, at the Isaac Taylor Community Center in Jerusalem.

Their local Smorodna *landsleit* followed them like children who had found a lost uncle. It was hot to travel with the extra passengers, even with the air conditioning, but they didn't mind. They all looked forward to the dedication of their building the following Sunday.

During their visit to the Kupat Holim's General Hospital in Beersheva, Frumele received a phone call from Malka Portugali at *Histadrut* Headquarters in Tel Aviv.

"*Chavera* Frumele, I have a telegram for you from Baltimore. Your husband has had a heart attack. He is in Sinai Hospital. I can make reservations for you to fly back to the States as soon as you are ready."

"I am ready now." Frumele whispered to Sholom what Malka had just told her, and he took the telephone.

"*Giveret* Portugali, I will go with Frumele. She hasn't been feeling well the last few days, since we left Poland, and she shouldn't be alone now. Please, make reservations for me, also."

By the time the coach returned from Beersheva, Malka Portugali was waiting for them at the hotel. Their suitcases were packed, the hotel bill was paid, and a *Histadrut* driver was waiting to take them to Ben Gurion Airport.

"*Chavera* Frumele, I hope your husband will have a speedy recovery. We will send you tapes and pictures of next Sunday's dedication ceremony."

Frumele thanked Malka for her help. She was upset and felt guilty for not being at home with her husband. When they arrived at the airport, the *Histadrut* driver made sure that inspection of their luggage would not delay their departure.

16

THE EL AL FLIGHT was only half full, so there were enough seats for Sholom and Frumele to stretch out and sleep, but Frumele was too upset and nervous to rest. She put her head on Sholom's shoulder and let her mind drift backwards while the plane was speeding towards New York.

"Do you feel like talking?" Sholom asked.

"About what?"

"About anything. We've got lots of time. Tell me about Oscar."

"Well, we dated for several months. One evening, when we'd gotten back after a dinner, it was pouring, and I suggested that he wait until the rain stopped. Oscar asked me about my plans for the future, and if I'd thought about getting married. I told him that if the right man ever came along, I'd consider it.

"He asked me if I liked him, and I said that I did. He said that, as I knew, he was much older than me, and he was still mourning his wife and children. He told me that since he'd met me, his depression was much less, and that his doctor had commented on how much more cheerful he'd become. He asked me to consider marrying him and going to America with him and Jacob.

"I said that I would. I liked Oscar, and trusted him,

and I wanted to get far away from the slaughterhouses of Europe.

"With the help of the Governor's office and some Maryland congressmen, Oscar got all my entry papers and Jacob's adoption documents cleared in two months, and we came to Baltimore. My first request was that we move out of his home. It had lots of room, but there were reminders of Lazar and Sally everywhere. Every corner of the house was filled with *tzatskes* (knick-knacks). Oscar was reluctant to move, but he understood my feelings. We found the much more modest home where we live now. Oscar helped me choose new furniture, and we settled down.

"He returned to his consulting practice, advising government agencies, trade unions, and business people how to invest their pension funds and stocks, and what insurance to buy. I attended night school at Baltimore Polytechnic Institute to learn English. We hired a tutor for Jacob, to prepare him for school. I began meeting Smorodna compatriots, some distant relatives of my mother's, in the Rotstein Family Circle, and slowly I became absorbed into my new Baltimore environment.

"During the third year of our marriage I gave birth to a son, and Oscar was in seventh heaven. When I agreed to name him Bernard, after Oscar's father, Oscar cried tears of joy, and bought me an expensive ring. He was a wonderful father — he used to sit for hours rocking the baby and singing lullabies. He'd find every opportunity to stay home to help Jacob with his school work and play with Bernie.

"Oscar insisted that the boys have a traditional Jewish education. Both attended Beth Tefilo Day School, and became *Bar Mitzvah*. I was in the Parent/Teacher Association.

"After Oscar's sixtieth birthday, I begged him to slow

down. He had begun to complain of chest pains, but the competition in the insurance business was too fierce for Oscar to slack off. He'd meet with private clients almost every evening, attend meetings with union leaders until late at night, and come home tired and complaining of fatigue. He'd fall asleep reading his mail or watching television.

"Jacob went to the University of Maryland, and Bernie was involved with high school activities. Our nest was emptying, and I was bored and lonely. Sisterhood at our synagogue did not appeal to me, probably because I was raised without religion.

"I went to several meeting of the Workmen's Circle, but I felt like I was in an old age home. Everyone was in their seventies and eighties. So I started to read and to write some poetry, maybe my memoirs, just to keep occupied. I'd sit up at night watching television or listening to the radio, because when I finally fell asleep, I'd have nightmares.

"Smorodna haunted me, and all this was reflected by my health. I became more irritated, nervous, depressed, and moody. I developed a guilt complex. Why did I leave Smorodna, and why did I survive? What right did I have to this tranquil life in the United States when all my dear ones had perished? I thought of suicide. I wanted to atone for my sins towards my parents, and towards Oscar. I felt that I'd been shamefully dishonest with him; that I'd deceived him, and had taken advantage of his goodness and his tragic situation. I hadn't married him for love, but just to get away from the blood-soaked earth of Europe.

"And what did I give Oscar in return? Jacob grew up a loner. He had been a moody, unhappy boy at the Vladeck Children's Home and cried a lot at night. He would never talk to us about his nightmares, and he refused to get therapy.

Bernie is a good student, but his interests are limited — sports, television, and comic books. Also, he spends too much time with the wrong kind of friends in pool halls.

"Maybe Oscar should have married an American-born woman who would have shared his interests in sports and in card games. I respect him, and I try hard to understand and please him.

"I've spoken only briefly with Oscar about my feelings, and he has pleaded with me to meet with his friend, Dr. Nathan Drazin, the rabbi of Shaare Tfiloh Congregation. I felt some apprehension meeting with a rabbi, you know, since I spent my tender years in *Bundist* schools, but Dr. Drazin did not look like our Smorodner Rav — no long beard and earlocks. He was a tall, clean-shaven man with a smiling face adorned by a mustache, and twinkling eyes showing through rimless glasses.

"I was impressed by Dr. Drazin's huge library which spanned three walls of his study, full of religious books in Hebrew, English, and Yiddish. The remaining wall displayed framed diplomas from Columbia, Johns Hopkins and Yeshiva Universities. Also displayed were awards and citations in Hebrew and English from Israel Bonds, Jewish National Fund, Associated Jewish Charities, Talmudical Academy, and many other organizations.

I revealed to Dr. Drazin the pain, my inner-struggle, how difficult it had been for me to live with the unresolved emotional problems, to rid myself of the constant nightmares of my past.

Oscar, I told him, is a well intentioned husband, close, warm and loving. I am unrewarding to him and detached from Jacob and Bernie, my own children. I am not able to feel close to anyone except survivors, only they can understand the inner struggle, the anger I have to live with. But I want so much to be a good wife to Oscar and a good mother to Jacob and Bernie. It is very important to me that I not hurt Oscar and the people around me. I always tried to understand how Oscar feels, to face his generosity and loving goodness. I taught my sons, Jacob and Bernie, to love people, when myself I still carry rage, malic for the murderers of my parents, my people. . . . This is the way I am. I know, dear rabbi, that I am not consistent, a very fallible nature.

It is hard for me to go on living, hurting Oscar, my children and the people around me. . . but what can I do?

My nights are overwhelmed by dreams of my burning home town, the extermination of my people and the guilt feeling, why did I survive?

"Why did I leave the children at the Vladeck Children's Home for my pure selfish reasons?"

My voice was dulled by melancholy and I started to cry. . . . Dr. Drazin listened to me with complete attention. I was appalled by his silence, he had not uttered a single word during my tirade, my sharing of my feelings.

"Dr. Drazin had a remarkable ability to listen without judgement, stopping me only to ask a question, clarify a thought, or make a point. I told him the story of my life, omitting nothing, telling things I've rarely shared with anyone, including Oscar.

"Dr. Drazin responded in a subdued voice, almost in a whisper, sympathy glinting in his eyes:

"Thank you for coming and sharing your thoughts with me. I am an American, born in this country. I spent my early years in Ottawa, Canada. You see this library? There are many volumes about the Holocaust. Absolutely nothing in print can truly depict the horrors you have experienced, or those of other survivors. No one can answer the intellectual and religious questions that torment your soul."

"Rabbi Drazin told me, 'In one of my books, I dealt with the subject of love in our lives. Of course, I would never suggest that the Holocaust was made in heaven, but, since you mentioned that you had been raised on Mendele, Peretz, and Sholom Aleichem, you can find in the Peretz stories the inspiration that may draw you out of the past; not that you can or should forget, but you may find a purpose and reason to go on. In Peretz story: *If Not Higher* he tells you that helping a poor woman is a higher achievement than personally ascending to heaven. Couldn't this lesson be significant in your case? . . . Helping Oscar to regain his health after such a tragic loss, adopting Jacob, giving birth to and raising Bernie — all these things are a high achievement, helping others, while carrying the scars of the past and the memories of your parents.

"All of us must never forget what was done to our people. We, therefore, have an absolute obligation to help our Jewish homeland absorb survivors, Jews from lands of oppression. We must also pay more attention to our own children, to better plan for their futures." Dr. Drazin continued. "There are so many organizations that can use your help — charitable institutions, hospitals, old age homes, and schools. Come join us and you will find fulfillment and meaning in your life, in your survival.'

"I told Dr. Drazin that social gatherings, meetings, and parties annoy me, because I am caught up in thinking mostly about my past. I find Oscar's hobbies meaningless. I sympathize with his frustration with me. I respect him, and I try very hard to understand and to please him. Dr. Drazin's response was 'There are people who serve humanity with words, and there are people who are praying with deeds. . . . What matters is that they are helping each other. . . . For this reason alone it is worth living.'

"I can say to you, Sholom, that the visit to Dr. Drazin did me some good. I realized that I did indeed love Oscar, for all that he has done for me, for our sons. But I know that there is something missing from our relationship. The closeness that I read about in magazines, the closeness that I feel towards you . . . "

17

THE EL AL STEWARDESS served dinner. Frumele drank only orange juice. Sholom ate salad, drank a Coke, and then put their dishes on the empty seats.

"Would you like to rest now?"

"Are you tired of listening to me?"

"Don't say that. You know I want to know all about you. I have the notes you sent me, but you've never told me about your life here, with Oscar. Please, go on."

"Your coming into my life and our Ramat Gan project pulled me out of my melancholy mood. Oscar noticed the change in me right away, and was so happy. I had more energy and put more enthusiasm into soliciting funds for the project. I wasn't afraid to visit the black neighborhoods where Smorodna survivors have grocery stores. My feelings of guilt about my parents lessened with every new solicitation I made. I'd come home exhausted, hug Oscar, and be so happy that I'd raised $3,000 that day.

"Our daily meetings and phone conversations did me a world of good. When you talked about Chanele and Treblinka, I'd relive my own life, in Lodz, Cracow and Paris. Yes, we often argued, but we'd make up quickly. I so enjoyed our trips together, singing Yiddish songs."

Sholom muttered, "Bettsie doesn't like my Yiddish songs. She always says, 'Try to sing in English, so we can all understand.' I feel more and more of an estrangement from her, since I began working on our project. I remember that when we were finally able to present Dr. Herman Seidel with a check for the full amount of the project, and all the Smorodna compatriots were invited to the *Histadrut* dinner, Bettsie refused to come. When we planned the mission to Poland and Israel for the dedication, I asked her several times to come with us, and again she refused to join us. She insisted that she had no desire to see Smorodna or our project."

Frumele was tired, and kept saying over and over to herself, "I hope I won't be too late. Oh, God, if You are in Heaven, save my Oscar and I will promise to believe in You."

She slept for awhile, but awoke when the stewardess came around with a list of tax-free Israeli products. She went to the lavatory, washed her face, and came back to her seat.

"What are you thinking about, Sholom?"

"I think that our project made better people out of us, better Jews and better Americans."

"And I think that I now believe in destiny. It was *bashert* (destined) that we meet."

"I hope that we will remain friends. I will miss you, Frumele."

"And I'll miss you."

"Let me tell you, at the Gesher Haziv guest house, I really had to restrain myself from knocking on your door. I couldn't fall asleep that night. The way you kissed me, I just wanted to be with you, but I . . . "

"Why didn't you?"

"I was afraid of what it might lead to."

"I wanted you, too, but I've learned to control my feelings, and I'm faithful to Oscar."

"I feel the same way. I've never been unfaithful to Bettsie, but so often lately I've thought just how beautiful you are, how much you mean to me, but I was afraid to touch you. Isn't this crazy and irrational?"

"When it comes to emotions, there is no rationality. I'll be honest with you. So many times I've dreamed we were together, holding each other, and I've told myself that this was not love, but lust. Now I realize that what we have is pure, honest friendship."

"We're both trying desperately not to give in to temptation. It is unbearable, but the more that I think about us, the more I realize that we did the right thing, controlling our feelings."

Frumele pulled closer to Sholom, who was holding her hand with a firm, comforting grip.

"I want you to be happy with Oscar and with your children, but I hope you will continue to be my friend. We are 'one from a family, two from a *shtetl*' and continue to be my family."

Frumele managed a smile through her tears, and her voice was trembling. "The end of this trip will mark our farewell. I hope that Oscar will survive this ordeal. I will not fail him. I'm not as strong as you are because of my unfulfilled needs. I admire your moral strength, but I don't trust myself with you anymore. From now on, I will try to be a perfect wife and a perfect nurse to my husband. How selfish we are, just thinking of ourselves. It's good that we both had the courage all these months not to step over the line. Can you imagine what would have happened if you had come to me that night at the *kibbutz* hostel? No, I will not build my happiness on someone else's unhappiness. I belong with Oscar and my children, and you belong with Bettsie and your children. As for you and me, we are compatriots.

As you said, survivors *'Echod Me'ir ushtayim mimishpachah'* (one from a city, two from a family). No one can take away our friendship or our special feelings for one another."

They arrived in Baltimore. Sholom picked up their baggage and called a taxi for Frumele.

"Frumele, I hope Oscar is alright. I'll call you in the morning. If there is anything that you need, please call me."

"I will. All I need now is to be with Oscar. Good night."

Sholom took a taxi home.

18

THE TELEPHONE RANG, and the maid answered. "Schwartzman residence. May I help you?"

"Let me speak to Mrs. Schwartzman."

"I think she's sleeping."

"Please tell her to call her husband at the warehouse."

"Her husband is out of town, and won't be back until next Tuesday."

"This *is* her husband."

"Oh, Mr. Schwartzman, are you calling from Israel?"

"No, I'm here, in my office at the warehouse. How are the children?"

"They're fine. They're still at summer camp, in Annapolis."

"Please tell Mrs. Schwartzman to call me as soon as she wakes up."

"I will, Mr. Schwartzman."

Ten minutes later, Bettsie called back. "So, when did you get in?"

"Last night."

"Wasn't the dedication supposed to take place next Sunday?"

"We had to come home earlier. Oscar had a heart

attack, and is in Sinai Hospital in critical condition."

"Why didn't you come home?"

"I did. You were in bed — with Ralph."

Bettsie said nothing. "Haven't you anything to say?"

"I have a lot to say. This past year you've hardly spoken to me. Every day you've had meetings, or luncheons or dates with Frumele. I'm not blind. I know you're in love with her. I've spent many sleepless nights waiting for you, and where were you? For years I listened to you calling for Chanele in your dreams, and for the last six months all I've heard is Frumele. When was the last time you made love to me? When was the last time we went out for dinner? Even the children have noticed that you're never home, that you're always working on your damned project.

"Yes, I wanted company, and Ralph was here. Yes, we got drunk, and he slept here. So what? Were you and that Frumele angels? You've been travelling together now for three weeks, next door to each other in the same hotel. Tell me, honestly, since you've been raving about her all these months, was she as good in bed as I am? Do you love her? Do you want a divorce? Damn it, say something!"

"There is no need to argue. There's no need for you to insult me, and to use this kind of language."

"You're not even capable of getting angry. You're married to the factory, and you're in love with your compatriots. I've never complained, but I have needs, too." Bettsie started to cry.

"I'm coming home and we can talk."

Bettsie dropped the phone, and as it fell to the floor, it knocked over the family portrait of her with Sholom and the children.

Sholom parked the car, brought his suitcases in, and

slowly climbed the stairs.

Bettsie was still in her pajamas, still in bed, and still crying.

"Bettsie?"

"What?"

"Where do we go from here?"

"I don't care anymore."

"Do you want a divorce?"

"Do you?"

"No, I don't want to hurt our children."

"But you don't care if you hurt me, do you?"

"Whether you believe me or not, Bettsie, I really love you, even though I don't play tennis, or cards, or enjoy going to parties to drink."

"Ralph is not, was not, my lover. He's just an old friend who was here when we came back from a party, and we were both drunk. I was lonely, and just needed someone to be with. His wife is on vacation with their children in Atlantic City. We didn't plan it this way, and I'm sorry. I asked him to go home, but he was too drunk to drive. He promised not to touch me, and I didn't sleep with him. When I woke up and found him on your side of our bed, I yelled for him to leave."

Sholom sat on the edge of their bed. "Bettsie, I want you to know that Frumele is not my lover. She is devoted to Oscar. We are just good friends. We are compatriots from the same town, we have the same background, and we both felt the same obligation to help these people."

"Did you ever sleep with her?"

"No, I did not."

"Did you hug her? Hold her?"

"Yes, I held her when we visited the forest outside our

shtetl. We cried like two lost children. The whole delegation was crying."

"What do you want now? Shall I call my attorney?"

"Bettsie, it's up to you. If you want to out of this marriage, I will leave this morning. This is your home. I will even leave the factory. It was your father's gift to you and our children."

Bettsie burst into tears again. "The hell with the factory! I care about the children. This wasn't my fault. You've ignored me all year. I'm angry and hurt, and I ran out of patience with your never being here for us. So, yes, I started drinking, and then one thing led to another."

"I'm sorry, Bettsie, I really am, but I can't help it. This is the way I am. I care about my people. My whole family perished, except for me. Now these people, these survivors, are my family, too. I love you. I love our children. But please try to understand. Frumele and all the survivors from my *shtetl* are part of my family now."

Bettsie started to pick up the shattered glass and frame fragments from the broken family portrait on the floor. Sholom gently stroked her disheveled hair, when she turned suddenly turned her face towards his and, with both her fists, beat on his chest. With her hands shaking badly and tears running down her cheeks, she screamed at him, "You bastard! I was a faithful wife and a good mother, and you were a good husband and a devoted father. Look what your project has done to us! Giving money wasn't enough for you. You had to give away yourself and your family, too. Now you think I'm a whore. Say it, damn it! Bettsie Schwartzman is a prostitute. Say it!"

Sholom held her in his arms. "Go take a shower, get dressed and we'll visit the children. I brought some nice gifts for them."

Bettsie reluctantly agreed, and while she showered Sholom called the Intensive Care Unit at Sinai Hospital. A nurse told him that Oscar Glazman couldn't have any visitors, but that he could talk with Oscar's wife, who was right there.

"Who's this?"

"It's Sholom. How's Oscar?"

"He had a heart attack. They call it a myocardial infarction. He collapsed in his office and lost consciousness. It was fortunate that his secretary was right there. His breathing is almost normal now. There is no brain damage, just an abnormal heartbeat. I'm going to stay with him now. How are you?"

"Everything's under control. Bettsie and I are going to see the children now. Can I come to visit Oscar this evening?"

"Not yet, but I'll tell him that you called."

"Wish him a speedy recovery."

"I will. Thanks for calling, and say 'hi' to Bettsie."

While Bettsie made a quick lunch, Sholom showered and changed, called the factory, and brought the car from the garage. Two hours later, they arrived at the Habonim summer camp. They spent the rest of the day with the children, but after they kissed the children goodbye and walked back to their car, they drove home in silence. Sholom was able to forgive Bettsie for the previous night, but he was not able to forget. He felt guilty for neglecting Bettsie all those weeks, but seeing her with Ralph diminished his feeling of self-esteem. He felt that he'd been made a fool of, that he'd been taken advantage of, that Ralph and Bettsie had been amusing themselves at his expense. . . . Did it destroy his marriage? No, he knew that he still loved Bettsie and the children, but still, it hurt.

At dinner, Bettsie hardly spoke. Her expression was one of sadness and shame. She hardly touched her dinner, except for the wine. Sholom asked her if she'd go with him to visit Oscar, and she said she would.

19

Hello, is this where Pan Stefan Barski lives?"

"Yes, who's calling?"

"My name is Felicia Glazman. Is Mr. Barski in? I have regards from his sister Zoshia in Poland."

"Just a minute. I'll call my father."

"I am Stefan Barski. Can I help you?"

"Your sister Zoshia is a very close friend of mine. She saved me from the Nazis. I saw her in Jerusalem where she was being honored by the Israeli government for saving children, and I promised her that I'd call you as soon as I got home. Unfortunately, my husband had a heart attack, and it's taken me a little while to call you."

"I'm sorry to hear about your husband, but please tell me about Zoshia."

"She looks well. She misses you and your family, and hopes that someday she'll be able to visit you, or you'll be able to visit her in a free Poland.

Stefan Barski listened in silence to the strange voice, speaking in perfect Polish.

"Panie Barski, are you there?"

"I'm just stunned. Really, I'm overwhelmed. Can I come to see you, or would you give us the honor of visiting us?"

"It would be my pleasure to have you. Do you have a pen? This is my address and my phone number. Come Sunday after church for brunch."

"We can't come this Sunday. Our son, Anthony Joseph, is being ordained as a priest on Saturday by His Eminence Lawrence Cardinal Shehan." Felicia could hear the pride in his voice. "He will be offering his first Mass on Sunday at twelve-thirty at St. Dominic's in Baltimore. Would you come as our guest, representing my sister? I'd like Cardinal Shehan to meet you and hear about my Zoshia."

"My congratulations to all of you, but I can't make any commitments right now. I'm staying home with my husband while he's recuperating. *Panie* Stefan, is there anything you need, can I help you or your family right now?"

"Thank you. We're fine. My son is taken care of; my daughters are in high school; my wife has a part-time job in an office; and, well, I'm looking for a better job."

"Doing what?"

"Before the war I was a policeman, but I was wounded, and now I can't lift anything heavy, or do any physical work. When we lived in Chicago I worked as a night guard in an office building, but the winters were too cold for me, and we moved to Virginia, and then to Bowie, Maryland. I do odd jobs. The police can't hire me because of my disability, but we manage. Both my girls have part-time jobs. We all pitch in, and thank the Lord, we're not starving. We 're so glad to be here, in America. I just wish my sister could join us; she's such a good person."

"*Panie* Barski, I will help you find a job. I promise. I'll call you back soon. It was so good to talk with you. Congratulations again to your son and your family. *Dowidzenia!*"

◆ ◆ ◆

That same evening Frumele called back. *"Panie* Barski?"

"Please, call me Stefan."

"Stefan, would you accept a job as a guard in a furniture factory? It's not hard work; you just need to be alert and honest."

"I have good recommendations from every place I've ever worked. Where is this job located?"

"In Baltimore. On Hanover Street."

"There's just one problem. I don't have transportation."

"Do you have a driver's license?"

"Yes, but I don't have a car. We have an old station wagon, but it belongs to the church, and my son needs it."

"Don't worry. We'll get you a car, and pay the insurance. Call Sol Schwartzman at the Levinson Furniture Factory first thing tomorrow morning, no later than eight o'clock. Mr. Schwartzman knows all about your sister. He said that you can start right away."

"Pani Glazman, Felicia, I don't know what to say or how to thank you."

"The only thing to say is 'thank God for your sister Zoshia. She's a saint."

"I wish my wife and children could hear this."

"I will tell them what a wonderful sister you have. *Dowidzenia."*

"Uprzejmie dziekujemy (we kindly thank you)."

20

Theodore R. McKeldin, Mayor

March 4th

Mr. Sol Schwartzman, Chairman
Dinner Committee
Smorodna Holocaust Survivors
c/o Mr. Isaac Goldman, Exec. Sec.
Baltimore Jewish Committee of New Americans

Dear Mr. Schwartzman:

I am delighted to bring greetings to your Smorodna
Compatriots Dinner and to the Baltimore Jewish Committee of New Americans, that admirable group of
former displaced persons and concentration camp inmates who have made their home in Baltimore.

The United States has long been the land to which
oppressed people might look in time of trouble. I
pray that it might continue to be so, and I pray
that people like you, who have come to know and love
this nation despite its many problems, may continue
to proceed to its shores in difficult times.

Sincerely yours,

Theodore R. McKeldin, Mayor

PROCLAMATION

BY

MAYOR THEODORE R. MC KELDIN

DESIGNATING THE WEEK OF APRIL 4 THROUGH APRIL 10, 1965

AS

"LIBERATION WEEK" IN BALTIMORE

The year 1965 marks the twentieth year of the liquidation of the iniquitous Nazi concentration camps by the victorious Allied Armies.

Many individuals thus liberated from the jaws of death have found a haven of refuge and opportunity in the hospitable City of Baltimore and throughout the United States.

These new residents in our community have heroically and courageously rebuilt their shattered lives in our free, democratic and tolerant society.

These new citizens, enjoying the blessings of our community, are now an integral part of our citizenry and are making magnificent contributions to the business, cultural, professional, and educational life of our Municipality.

Ceremonies of thanksgiving and rededication are planned by the Maryland Committee for New Americans during the week beginning April 4, 1965.

NOW, THEREFORE, I, THEODORE R. MCKELDIN, MAYOR of Baltimore City, do hereby proclaim the week beginning April 4, 1965 as "LIBERATION WEEK" and I call on all the residents of this community to pause and rededicate themselves to the mandate imposed on us by George Wash-

ington when he wrote that "Everyone shall sit in safety
under his own vine and fig tree, and there shall be
none to make him afraid."

IN WITNESS WHEREOF, I
have hereunto set my hand
and caused the Great Seal
of the City of Baltimore
to be affixed this second
day of April, in the year
of Our Lord, one thousand
nine hundred and sixty-
five.

⎯⎯⎯⎯⎯⎯⎯⎯⎯
Mayor

Upon the return of the Smorodna Mission from Israel,
the Rotstein Family Circle arranged a welcome home dinner at the Bluefield North for the families and friends who
had supported their building campaign. The dinner was
attended by several hundred people, Smorodna compatriots
from the Baltimore-Washington area, community leaders
and representatives of the local and national *Histadrut* Campaign. Dr. Samuel Rosenblatt, Rabbi of Beth Tefilo Congregation, gave the invocation. He praised the Rotstein Family Circle, especially Sholom Schwartzman and Mrs. Oscar
Glazman, for their efforts on behalf of their *landsmen* in
Israel. Dr. Rosenblatt quoted the Bible:

> "You shall not harden your heart, nor shut your hand
> from your needy brother, but . . . lend him sufficient
> for his need."

Greetings came from the Mayor of Baltimore, Theodore
R. McKeldin, from Israel Stolarski of the National *Histadrut*
in New York, the Smorodner *landsmen,* in Ramat Gan, and

from the Associated Jewish Charities of Baltimore.

After the dinner Oscar, leaning on a cane, came over to Sholom. "Dear Sol, I personally want to thank you for what you've accomplished, and for what you've done for me and for my family. You gave my Frumele a new lease on life. As much as I missed her this past year, I understood the importance of what she was doing, and how much it meant to her. Truly, it gave new meaning to her life. Now that this campaign is over, I hope we'll remain friends and you will come often to visit us."

Frumele came over, took Oscar's arm and greeted Bettsie and Sholom warmly, but Bettsie's reaction was anything but warm. Her expression was one of fright and jealousy, and it gave Frumele a chilly reaction. She was surprised and hurt. Frumele said goodnight to Sholom and walked away in a hurry, hiding the tears in her eyes.

21

WEEKS PASSED. Sholom was home almost every evening with Bettsie and the children.

He tried to catch up on long-neglected letters and made an album of all the pictures and newspaper articles that had appeared over the last year in American and Israeli magazines about their project. There were no more phone calls, no more night meetings for him. During the day, he concentrated on his business, but the quiet of the evenings brought a strange melancholy, a let-down, and a sadness. He felt as if he'd reached the top of the cliff, and was looking down into a pit of loneliness and despair.

He longed for Frumele, her pleasant voice, her beautiful eyes, her wonderful and clever Yiddish expressions which she used even when she was criticizing him. When he held Bettsie in his arms he'd be careful not to call her Frumele or Chanele.

The images of Chanele and Frumele were now intermingled, and they followed him day and night. One day, at his office in the warehouse, Sholom picked up the phone and called Frumele. "How are you? How's Oscar?"

"We're fine. How is your family? It's nice of you to think about us, but why did you wait so long to call?"

Sholom said nothing for a few moments, but his heart was pounding.

"What happened? Did you fall asleep? Sweet dreams."

"Frumele, I'm not asleep. I can't get a moment's rest."

"Me either, but we have to be strong. We both have families."

"You're right but, still, I can't rest. I think of you day and night. I'm going to Florida for *Pesach,* so I called to wish you a Happy *Pesach.* Only God knows how much I miss you."

"I miss you, too, but we've talked about this before. I don't want to build my happiness on our families' unhappiness."

"Bettsie will find a better husband."

"But Oscar will not find a better wife, and my children will not find a better mother. Oscar gave me two beautiful sons, he helped me start a new life in freedom, away from the *farsholtene* (cursed European soil), and I'm repaying my debt to him. I'm going to nurse him with my devotion, my love, and my attention, day and night. I've even begun to join him for services at his *shul,* just to be with him and the children."

"I still find it difficult to pray to a God who allowed the gassing of a million and a half Jewish children, six million of our people. You know, I was not brought up in a religious house, and now I sit in the synagogue and listen to the Rabbi's sermons and sing songs with words of wisdom, but in my inner self, in my consciousness, I have *taynes* (complaints). I know the world's leaders were silent, but why was God silent? All this happened in God's world.

"I sit in the synagogue next to Oscar, I read the Hebrew prayers, I join in the singing, but my heart is crying.

The only thing that keeps me going is my preoccupation with Oscar."

"I'm not asking you to leave him. Couldn't we just see each other occasionally, just to sit and talk?"

"No, I don't think so. Believe me, this is just as difficult for me as it is for you, but I'm afraid that one thing will lead to another, and I'm not as strong as you are. I'm very grateful to you for what you've done, for me, for our *landsmen,* but it is very hard for me to see you and just be friends. I'll remember you for the rest of my life.

"Please call us from time to time. Oscar asks about you, but I've stopped going to Family Circle meetings because people have been asking too many questions, like how often we see each other. It's hard to hide our feelings for one another, and we've become fodder for gossip.

"Sholom, remember me as you saw me at our last Circle dinner, when we both had tears in our eyes. That was our goodbye. Have a happy *Pesach.*"

◆ ◆ ◆

Bettsie couldn't help but notice that Sholom had become moody and depressed, so his suggestion that they take a vacation to her parents' home in Hallendale, Florida pleased her immensely. They made reservations for Bettsie and the children to go at the start of Easter vacation, and for Sholom to join them on *Erev Pesach* (the eve of Passover).

While Bettsie and the children were gone, Sholom gave the maid a vacation, to go home to visit her family in South Carolina.

On Sunday afternoon, he decided to visit the Kornblitts,

landsmen from Smorodna, who owned a grocery store in a black neighborhood. It was a visit he had promised to make many months earlier. The Kornblitts lived on the first floor of an old, three-story, dilapidated apartment building, next door to their grocery store with its CocaCola sign, "Paul's Grocery."

The window was covered with iron bars that reminded Sholom of the bars in Treblinka. The weekly specials were written on hand-written signs in the window: pig tails, 15 cents a pound; neck bones, 15 cents a pound; turkey necks, 4 pounds for 99 cents.

A light spring rain was falling, and the street was deserted. Sholom parked his car and rang the bell at the side door. The iron bars on the doors and windows overwhelmed him with feelings of gloom.

Paul Kornblitt opened the door, his hair disheveled, his eyes sleepy, "Welcome, Sholom, what a surprise! Come in, come in. I fell asleep waiting for you. We're open late on Saturday, but we only stay open half a day on Sunday. Before I forget, did you lock your car?"

"No, why? I've got nothing in it."

"Sholom, in this neighborhood, if you don't lock your car it won't be there when you go out or, God forbid, even worse, there will be someone waiting for you in the back seat, with a knife."

Paul waited while Sholom went to lock his car, then asked if Sholom would like a tour of his "kingdom," his grocery store. "I just modernized the refrigeration and put in new shelves and meat cases."

Sholom followed Paul to the store, also protected with double iron bars. The smells of chicken and fish, fruits and vegetables were in the air. The shelves were full of canned goods, cereals, and cakes and cookies for Easter.

"This is my kingdom now. When I left Israel and the Lodziya textile factory, we settled here, in Columbus *Medinah* (America)."

"As long as you are happy, and making a living."

"We're making a living, but this isn't happy. The iron bars we didn't install because we wanted to, but because we had to. This is a dangerous place to be."

A middle-aged woman walked in. "Is this the way you greet guests? Come back to the house. I've made some tea."

"Sholom, this is my wife, Leah, my *Eishes-Chayil* (woman of valor). She's also from Lodz."

Sholom followed them to their small living room, decorated with a poster of the Carmel Mountains. Curtains over the windows covered the iron bars. Leah served tea and some Keebler cookies. Paul pointed to the picture on the wall with a sigh, "I'd hoped you'd come with your wife. I wanted Leah to meet her. We saw her picture in the "Jewish Times."

"She's in Florida now, with our children, visiting her parents. I'm going to join them on Friday. Paul, may I ask you, where did you go when you escaped from Smorodna?"

"Well, when we were ordered to clear out from our homes, we first gathered at the *Beis Midrash* yard, and then we escaped to Vilna. We lived there until June, 1941, when the *Wehrmacht* and their 185 divisions attacked the Soviet Union. I was working in a tailor's cooperative, and the Germans ordered all cooperative workers to a labor camp, to sew uniforms for the German army. *Heferingen* (SS women) were stationed there, and they were more cruel than some of the men. They carried flexible steel whips covered with plaited leather, and they used them.

"Our barracks were near Ponar. 47,000 Jews from Vilna were murdered there between June and November, 1941."

"How do you know all this?"

"We didn't know. The Germans kept telling us that the people were being transferred to factories, but in November a young girl — her name was Sara Menkes — was shot with a group of women and children. Somehow she was able to crawl out of the pit at Ponar, and then she walked all night to Vilna. She told anyone who would listen that 40,000 Jews had been killed and buried in ditches, but no one believed her; they called her a crazy lunatic.

"But Abba Kovner, the leader of the Vilna underground, believed her. A group of us escaped from the labor camp, went back to the ghetto, and joined the resistance. I was with the partisans until liberation. After the war I went to Germany and lived in a D.P. camp in Foehrenwald, where I met Leah. She had survived the ghetto, Ravensbrook concentration camp, and the detention camps in Cyprus. We left for Israel on the Exodus."

"And how did you adjust to being in America?"

Paul moved closer to Sholom. "I've just begun to realize how very precious Israel is to me. I dream every night about Lodziya and the factory where I worked. We didn't save any money, but we had a small, clean apartment and we had our Smorodner and Lodzer compatriots. I worked hard all week, but on *Shabbos* I was a king. We played cards, or went to a movie or a concert, but here we live in a jail. Leah's only sister, who lives in Randallstown, is afraid to come visit us, it's that dangerous."

"Don't criticize my sister. No one forced you to come here. You always complained that the factory work was too strenuous for you. You didn't like the Israeli climate; you thought the apartment was too small and the taxes were too high. In all your letters to my sister you begged her to send you papers. She helped you with money to buy this store, and you have more money in the bank now than you've ever had in your whole life. Suddenly you've become an Israeli patriot? I was the one who wasn't ready to leave Israel. The children loved their school and their friends."

Leah turned to Sholom, "Paul insisted that we try for a few years, save some money for a bigger apartment and a textile machine, and then return to Israel. Now, every time we have visitors, he blames my sister."

"Who said that I blame your sister? I just said that I was lonely here."

"You never want to go anywhere. We were invited to a dinner of the New Americans Club, and you didn't want to go; you were afraid that you'd have to close the store an hour early."

"I was scared to come home after dark."

Not wanting to be part of a family argument, Sholom excused himself, promised to come again, and wished them a Happy Passover.

◆ ◆ ◆

Waiting in line at the airport, Sholom heard the news on the radio that the Rev. Martin Luther King had been fatally shot at the Loraine Motel in Memphis. He quickly returned to his car and drove to the warehouse. He called Bettsie and told her that he decided to stay in Baltimore, and warned her to be careful, not to leave her parents' home and not to let the children swim in the ocean.

He went home, changed clothes and then the telephone rang. It was the fire department, calling to let him know that the warehouse was up in flames, but that they couldn't get to the flames because the neighborhood was full of snipers. All the warehouses on Hanover and the surrounding streets were being looted, several police and firefighters had been hurt, and one had been killed. Sholom was told not to come to the warehouse. The death of Rev.King enraged the nation's blacks, triggering riots all over Baltimore. Bands of youg blacks set fires and looted stores.

The Governor, Spiro Agnew, ordered the National Guard to mobilize 6,000 guardsmen. Everyone was told to stay put. White people were being pulled from their cars, stabbed, assaulted, and robbed.

Sholom called the guard at the warehouse, but there was no answer. He called the factory and Stefan Barski answered. "All the other warehouses on Hanover Street are being looted, but no one's going to touch this place. There were looters here, but I got on the loud speaker and said that I was armed, that there were fifty black brothers who work here, and that to loot this factory would be robbing them of their livelihoods. They called me white shit, but they left."

The telephone rang again. It was Oscar. "Just wanted to know if you were home. I saw the warehouses on Hanover Street on television. Everything's up in flames. Do you have enough insurance?"

"I think so."

"How are Bettsie and the children?"

"They're fine. They went to Florida to have *Pesach* with my in-laws. How do you feel?"

"Better, thanks."

"How's Frumele?"

"She's fine. She's busy this week delivering Passover packages from the Associated Jewish Charities to needy families in the area."

"Thanks for calling. Please give Frumele my regards, and I wish you a Happy Passover."

"Sholom, don't give up."

"I won't, but this is so discouraging."

◆ ◆ ◆

As the riots intensified, it was dangerous to leave the house. The situation in Baltimore became perilous. Sholom couldn't go to the factory, not in his own car, not with his black driver, who was afraid to pick him up or drive with a white man in the back seat.

Sholom called Bettsie, telling her again how sorry he was that he couldn't be with her and the children for the *Seder.* "It's too dangerous to drive to the airport. I love you, and I miss you. Say 'Good *Yom Tov*' to your parents for me."

That evening he lit two candles, opened a box of *matzoh,* filled a cup with Shapiro wine, opened the *Haggadah,* and read the blessing over the wine. It was salty from his tears.

Leah Kornblitt called late that night. "Sholom," she cried, "they killed my Paul. He tried to resist that gang of hoodlums, and they killed him. He is at Levinson Funeral Home, and I'm at my sister's in Randallstown. The police brought me here. Two black policemen.

The funeral's on Sunday. God gave me a grim *Pesach.* I know it's *Yom Tov,* but please come."

"Of course, I'll be there."

◆ ◆ ◆

Sholom knew how close he was to his compatriots. Bettsie had blamed him for giving so much time to his *landsmen,* for the project. Now his years of hard work had gone up in flames. Everything was gone. Would he be able to go back and rebuild, to work with the same black people who had killed his friend Paul?

For years he had deceived himself into believing that he had been accepted into the Jewish establishment in Baltimore, yet there had not been one phone call from any of the board members of the various organizations he had served and supported. Only Oscar had called, and he was sure that it was Frumele who had asked him to call.

He thought to himself, "Why am I looking for scapegoats? Why do I blame Bettsie for my neglecting Paul Kornblitt and our other compatriots? It's my own fault." He couldn't sleep, so he turned the television on. He missed Bettsie and the children, and downtown Baltimore was still burning.

22

ON THE WAY to the Levinson Funeral Home, Sholom remembered his father, of blessed memory, quoting Sholom
Aleichem, "Life is a blister on top of a tumor, and a boil on
top of that." The life of Paul Kornblitt was full of blisters
and tumors, and it was a boil on top of that which killed
him.

Despite the danger of driving on Reisterstown Road,
and this Sunday being the second day of Passover, the funeral home was full of people, survivors of the Holocaust,
two black policemen, Smorodna *landsmen,* and friends of
the Kornblitt children, Rosalie, Michael, and Aaron.

Sholom had met Rosalie when he and Frumele had
addressed a meeting of the Baltimore Committee of New
Americans at the home of Jean and Isaac Goldman. Rosalie
had been more interested in learning details about the life
of her grandfather, the Dayan of Smorodna, than about the
Ramat Gan Housing Project. She said then that her father
never talked about his life, and especially not his experiences during the Holocaust. She only knew that her grandfather, Rabbi Joel Kornblitt, had died in the flames of the
Smorodna *Beis Midrash,* during the first week of the Nazi
occupation.

"Our father forced us to leave Israel against our will. When we first came to Baltimore, I wanted to go right back to Israel, but I decided to finish school first. As soon as I graduated, I moved out of the house and took a job. I had made some friends among other *Yordim* (families who came from Israel), and I moved in with them.

"I was angry with my father, and began dating gentile boys. Now I've settled down. I'm working in a law office, I go to night school, and I hope to return to Israel."

"And your brothers?"

"Michael is wild. He won't study. He doesn't want to work in the store. He asked our father for money for plane tickets to go back to Israel, so he can join the IDF (Israeli Defense Forces). He considers Israel his home, and he doesn't want to be called a deserter.

"But my parents have insisted that both boys first graduate from high school before they go back to Israel. I know that our parents both love us dearly, but they still have this European *shtetl* mentality, that he is the father, and he's always right."

Before Rosalie left that night, she gave Frumele an envelope with five $20 bills. "Sorry this is so little, but it's all I can afford right now. I'm making this donation in memory of my grandparents."

Now, a year later, he saw Rosalie again, sitting next to Leah, Michael, and Aaron, at the funeral of her father. According to the *Baltimore Evening News*, "Paul Kornblitt, 49, was fatally beaten by a band of hoodlums last Friday afternoon, while getting ready to close his store on the eve of Passover."

The rabbi commented that it was ironic that a former partisan, a fighter in Israel's War of Independence, the son of a Dayan, Paul Kornblitt, was carrying on what was also the ideal of Rev. Martin Luther King, in whose name Paul was murdered."

Because of the holiday, there was no eulogy, just a few remarks. They continued with the 23rd Psalm, and the memorial prayer. There was no rending of the garment. The Rabbi followed the coffin and the service was over.

On his way home, Sholom was numb with shock. Here was Paul, his *landsman,* whom he'd known since they were children. They'd played hide-and-seek in the Smorodna *Cheder* yard. Just last week he'd been at Paul's house, and now Paul was gone.

Sholom thought, "If only I'd called him and invited him and Leah for the *Seder,* would he be alive now? What will happen to Leah? Will she be able to open the store again, and face her customers? Will Michael and Aaron help her now? Would he be able to go back to the factory and face his own workers? How many of his employees participated in the riots? How many of them looted the warehouse?"

23

HE CAME HOME and called Bettsie. She was out playing tennis, and the children were in the pool. Sholom spoke to his father-in-law, "How are you, Pop?"

"Oh, I'm fine," he responded sweetly. "We missed you at the *Seder,* and we're worried about you. Bettsie says you're in a melancholy mood. There's no reason for that. You have everything any man could ever want in his life. The warehouse? You're not the only one who suffered a loss. Our insurance policy will cover most of it. So you'll pay less taxes this year. Fires have happened before. Sit back and wait a few days. See what others do. My advice is to leave everything, come down here, and stay until the children have to go back to school next Monday."

"Thank you for the invitation, but I'd rather stay here. I hope to go to the factory tomorrow. There are lots of problems to sort out. The insurance people want records and there are papers to be filled out for unemployment compensation for the workers. Isn't this a cruel joke! We lost a warehouse with millions of dollars worth of merchandise, and we still worry about our employees. Maybe one of them was the one who set fire to our warehouse?

"Not all of them did it to loot. Some of them were

angry over the death of Dr. King, and keep in mind the numbers of blacks who *didn't* participate in the riots. Don't forget that Dr. King preached non-violence and racial harmony."

"There was no racial harmony on the streets of Baltimore this week. Hundreds of my fellow survivors were wounded and lost their grocery stores to fires and looters. And one of my *landsmen* was killed. I just came back from his funeral. He was my age."

"I'm so sorry. We heard on television this morning that thirty-one people have died in this violence nationwide."

"Let me ask you something. I've noticed lately that Bettsie has been drinking a lot. She frequently has a wine glass in her hand, and refills it often. She's very moody, and when I ask her what's wrong, she cries. Have you noticed anything?"

"No, just that she misses you and wishes that you were here with us. I still think you should come down, even for just a few days."

"Let me take care of some things at the factory. I'll call her tomorrow. It was good to talk to you. Say hello to everyone for me, and Happy Passover."

Sholom realized that he had no Passover food in the house, except for eggs, *matzoh,* wine, and gefilte fish. He poured himself some orange juice and sat down in his chair to think about Bettsie. Since he'd gotten back from the mission to Israel, the relationship between them had seemed so fragile, almost official, and very correct. Yes, she continued to be a devoted mother and a caring wife, but the warmth and intimacy he had known before was missing. Was it Bettsie, or was it his fault? Were his feelings for Frumele interfering? Was it jealousy? Was Bettsie yearning for Ralph as he was yearning for Frumele?

Then it dawned on him, the difference in what he felt for the two women. Bettsie was his wife, the mother of his children, the woman he shared his love with for almost two decades. Frumele, on the other hand, was the image of Chanele, of the sister he never had, a reminder and a symbol of his past, his *shtetl.*

He got up and opened a jar of gefilte fish. And then he called Frumele, *"Gut Yom Tov* (Happy Passover)! How are all of you?"

"Gut Yom Tov Gut Yor! You didn't go to Florida?"

"No, I stayed here."

"What are you doing with yourself?"

"I went to a funeral this morning. Paul Kornblitt. Do you remember him?"

"I remember his daughter. We read about it in the Evening News. Oscar went to the synagogue for services, and I went to Sinai Hospital to visit some of our survivors. Two are in intensive care, one in a coma, and the other had a heart attack. Several others were beaten while trying to defend their stores from the mobs. One man was delirious. He was shouting, *"Pogromtchiks!* Why us? We were good to you. We sympathized with your struggle against discrimination, against segregation. We gave you food on credit."

Just to listen to them, it breaks my heart. It's such a nightmare. These horror stories are a reminder of Smorodna, of the arrival of the Germans. One of our *landsmen,* Blimboymer, was beaten with a baseball bat. His wounds are so deep that his doctors assumed that he'd been shot. He recognized his assailants — they had been his customers. I walked from room to room in the hospital, and looking at the maimed faces, the bandaged arms and legs, and I was back in 1939 again.

"Most of the victims are white, and most of the whites

are Jews, and most of the Jews are our own survivors. Watching them, I was thinking, what would they do when they are released from the hospital? Would they go back to their grocery stores? What can we do for them? Some of them have no place to go; they've lost everything."

"Frumele, I agree with you. We have to help them. Tomorrow I'll call Harry Greenstein at the Associated Endowment Fund office and Jacob Edelman at City Hall and see if we can establish a fund to provide immediate assistance."

"If you want, Oscar is willing to help. We talked about it today. He's had experience in this field."

"I'll call him after I speak with Harry and Jacob. Frumele, I saw Sandra at the funeral. She was alone."

"I know, Alyosha is in the Taylor Manor Hospital. I talk to her very often."

"Why didn't you call me?"

"It is not exactly the kind of news we enjoy spreading. He suffers from manic depression."

"Does Sandra need some help?"

"Not financially. She sold the roofing business and she receives a pension from Germany. His disability insurance pays the hospital costs. What she needs is friends, someone to talk to her. She visits Alyosha twice weekly."

"Is there any hope that Alyosha will recuperate?"

"When you lost all your family, your wife, and child, it is not easy to recuperate. It's hard to keep your sanity."

"We all followed the same routes, didn't we?"

"Some of us are stronger than others. Some of us have children, relatives. Alyosha has nothing but Sandra, and she is restless, hurt, always brooding. Sandra told me that just before liberation, she was beaten with a sledgehammer by a guard in Ravensbroock for scavenging for food in the garbage dumps. Theirs is a tragic, complicated situation. You know, Sholom, at the same time, she is such a *gute neshomeh* — such a generous soul. Every time she finds a family in need, the black families who worked for Alyosha, even total strangers, she buys food baskets and delivers them to their doorsteps. *Nu?* Can you understand this? *Nu, genug!* Enough! If I say one more word, I will start crying. Sholom, have a good holiday." Frumele hung up the telephone.

Sholom siged. Dear God, he thought, why such punishment? He was suddenly aware of tears falling down his cheeks. Were they for Paul? . . . for Alyosha and Sandra? . . . for Dr. Martin Luther King, Jr.? . . . or for his *landsmen* altogether?

24

On the flight to Florida, Sholom thought about what Rabbi Drazin had said at his wedding, "The act of sexual union is holy and pure. The Lord created all things in accordance with His wisdom and whatever He created cannot possibly be shameful or ugly. When a man is in union with his wife in a spirit of holy matrimony, of holiness and purity, the Divine Presence is with them. Marriages are made in heaven." Many times over the years these words by Rabbi Drazin had come to mind. He remembered them now on his way to see Bettsie and his children. The traumatic experiences of the last ten days, the riots and looting, the murder of Paul Kornblitt, and the fire in his warehouse had shattered his nerves.

Still, alone with his thoughts, he missed Bettsie. No, it was not shameful and ugly to desire his wife, even in a situation like this, and he thought about his first dates with her.

♦ ♦ ♦

When he began to attend social events at the Jewish Community Center on Monument Street, he felt like an alien from another planet. His English was limited and he was too shy to open his mouth. Girls giggled at him every time he said anything. He was fortunate to have a job, a clean bed, and his health. He ate foods he'd never dreamed of, and was going to night school, but he was sad and lonely. He dreamed about his father and Chanele, and wondered if life was worth living.

He remembered his *Cheder* years, and his Rabbi quoting the Bible, "As for man, his days are as grass. The wind passes over him and he is gone, and his place knows him no more." No one knew him or paid any attention to him until he met Bettsie at the Center. He was impressed with her subtle way of speaking to him. She showed a sincere interest in his background, and there was a humility about her that fascinated him.

They spoke about the Russian blockade of Berlin and the earthquake in Japan. Sholom shared with her the latest news from Israel which he'd heard on the radio that morning, that "after fierce fighting, the *Hagganah* forces liberated Haifa from the Arabs and their German-Nazi helpers."

He'd describe his day to Bettsie: Travel by streetcar to the Comfi factory, study English while eating lunch, travel again by streetcar to his rented room, have canned foods for dinner, and go to night school. This was the rhythm of each day, except Saturday and Sunday.

And Bettsie would describe her daily routine to Sholom: Morning exercise, light breakfast, ride with her father to his office to help with the mail, talk with school friends on the phone, lunch at a restaurant close to the factory or delivered from a nearby deli. Sometimes she would eat alone while reading a book, or go with the bookkeeper, Ralph, to play tennis. She liked movies with Judy Garland or Rita

Hayworth, and television shows with Milton Berle. Her mother was active in Hadassah, and she joined Junior Hadassah. Her group was not too intellectual, but more into social and charitable work. She liked dancing, and once a week came to the Center with Ralph to dance. They were friends, but not ready to go steady.

She told him of her enjoyment of nature, the flowers and trees, the scent of fresh-cut grass. She liked to swim, and then rest in the sun with a good book. She drove a sports car, but admitted to not liking to drive. She'd crashed into a fence the first night she had her car, and felt that she'd never feel secure driving at night again.

Her openness and friendliness had given him the courage to ask her for another date, and after several dates, she got up the courage to ask him why he was always so sad. He told her that his world had crumbled, his youth had cracked, that although he was in America, his thoughts were still in Europe. He told her that he was troubled about his future, and a stranger to his past. "I wonder whether I have a right to live, to be happy, when all my family and friends have perished so cruelly. Sometimes," he said, "everything around me seems so absurd, and I ask myself if there is a reason for living."

Bettsie had answered that she didn't know what to tell him, for "who am I to give you advice on how to cope with your sadness? My words are inadequate to give you counsel or suggestions on how to live with your horrible memories, what was done to you and your family, to our people in Europe." She admitted that she was not a very religious person, but she felt that "there must be a reason why God wanted you to survive, why you were spared. Maybe you were destined to do something good, something great, or perhaps just to live and tell your story to young Jews like me who know so little about what happened to Jews in Europe." She thanked him for sharing his thoughts with her, and said she hoped they'd meet again.

♦ ♦ ♦

Almost twenty years had passed since they were married. Despite their different habits, backgrounds, and social interests, they enjoyed their children and each other's company.

Bettsie did everything to make him happy, to ward off the melancholy which befell him from time to time. She intentionally hid from him all news of the Holocaust which came in the mail. If a donation was requested, she'd mail one out, but did not show him the letters depicting the horrors committed by the Nazis.

It was only when he started the Smorodna campaign that she felt neglected. She was hurt when he'd run off to meetings with Frumele, and felt that a meaningful contribution to the project would be enough, but to give away his days and nights at her expense and that of her children was too much for her to bear.

It had taken her years to get used to his nightmares, his calling out "Chanele, Chanele" in his sleep, but her dignity was assaulted when he began to call out "Frumele" instead. She hid her jealousy by indulging in too much wine and too many hours of tennis, until she'd injured her arm and shoulder.

Since his return from Israel, he noticed that she seemed to crawl into his arms, holding on to him more affectionately than he had remembered in years. One night she

asked him if he still loved her, and he said that he did. She
confessed that she'd been deceitful, that she had lost her
self-respect the night Shalom had found her with Ralph. "I
thought that you were unfaithful to me, and I was terribly
jealous, but I want you to believe me, that nothing happened between Ralph and me that night."

"I know."

"How do you know?" she asked.

Shalom explained that after he had received Ralph's
letter of resignation, Ralph also sent him a note explaining
that he and Bettsie were too drunk to do anything, and
that in the morning Bettsie had been so distressed, she had
chased him out of the house.

"Did you believe him?"

"Yes, I believed both of you. I understood that this was
as much my fault as it was yours. Let's not talk about it
anymore."

◆ ◆ ◆

Bettsie and the children were waiting for him at the
Miami airport. On the way to Bettsie's parents' home,
Jimmie drove, and Eve sat up front with him. Lorna and
Bettsie sat on either side of Sholom in the back seat, resting
their heads on his shoulders. Sholom noticed that Bettsie
looked pale and had dark shadows under her eyes.

"Are you feeling well?"

"Why do you ask?"

"Because you look pale, and very tired. Are you still
playing a lot of tennis?"

"I play one or two games a day. I get tired from the
sun being so strong here."

"Maybe you should see your doctor?"

"If you insist."

"I'm concerned."

"I'm glad."

"What are you so glad about?"

"That you're concerned about my health."

"Don't talk foolishly. You and the children are all I have."

"How's the factory?"

"We'll talk about that later."

♦ ♦ ♦

When they returned to Baltimore, Sholom took Bettsie to see their family doctor, who found a lump in Bettsie's breast and immediately performed a biopsy. "Fear just wastes your energy," he said. "We have found this early, and that's good. I'm going to send you to Johns Hopkins to see a surgeon."

They were devastated, and stood there stunned. Always a strong man, Sholom felt his knees trembling. Choking back tears, Bettsie held Sholom's face in her hands and told him, "Not a word to the children or to my parents. Not yet. Do you hear?"

They came home, and Bettsie went upstairs, pretending to sleep. After awhile she came down, but had no appetite. She went back upstairs and turned on the television, but paid little attention to it. She had no pain, but cried most of the evening. Sholom tried to comfort her, his voice soft, his hand caressing her hair. "Bettsie, dear, can you hear me?"

"Yes, Sol, I'm so scared. Why did you tell the children?"

"They're adults; they knew something was wrong. Why hide the truth from them?"

"I hope you didn't tell my parents."

"I didn't, and I won't until after the surgery."

She took his hand, and touched it with her lips. Sholom was crying. *"Mir far deine bainer* (I wish I could take your illness)."

"Stop crying. You've always been such a brave man."

"Darling, I'm so frightened."

"We have to be strong, and go on with our lives. I want you to be with me tomorrow, and after this is over."

"Bettsie, you know you haven't eaten all day?"

"The doctor told me not to eat anything after six o'clock tonight. Sol, no matter what happens, I want you to know that I love you, that I have from the first moment we met at the Jewish Community Center." She smiled, and held back her tears. "When I look back on our lives, we've no reason to complain. Our children gave us much *nachas* (joy). We've been very lucky." When he left the room, Bettsie tossed and turned. She had used her wits to try to cheer up Sol, but she herself needed encouragement.

♦ ♦ ♦

Bettsie was taken to surgery the next morning, with Sholom and the girls at the hospital, supporting each other. Jimmie was at the warehouse, overseeing the installation of new lifting machinery, scheduled for delivery that morning. After two hours, the chief surgeon appeared, and asked Sholom to come into his office. "We removed the tumor, and it was malignant. Your wife will need chemotherapy after the incision heals. The operation took so long because we used a new surgical method; we did not remove her breast, but cleaned out the tumor and the underlaying muscles around her lymph nodes."

"What about her depression? She won't eat."

"As she recuperates from the surgery, the depression will slowly diminish. Your family doctor will prescribe an anti-depressant which she can take with her juice in the morning."

♦ ♦ ♦

Sholom left the running of the factory to Jimmie and the managers. He settled with the insurance company for the damages to the warehouse, and mostly stayed home with Bettsie. Eva and Lorna, students at Loyola College and the University of Maryland, were home every evening and, after doing their school work, sat with their mother while their father was busy furnishing a new warehouse in Baltimore County, near the railroad tracks in Reisterstown.

Sholom attended a conference at the Baltimore mayor's office to discuss plans to help the victims of the riots. He met with Harry Greenstein, Director of the Associated Endowment Fund, and gave a substantial donation to the Special Fund, set up to help the grocery owners who lost their small businesses and homes in the riots. Frumele and Oscar Glazman ran the emergency campaign among the members of the Baltimore Committee of New Americans. He felt that his place was now to be with Bettsie.

25

BETTSIE STAYED AT JOHNS HOPKINS HOSPITAL for eight days with two private-duty nurses. Sholom was there every day, as were her parents and her children. When she came home, Jimmie's study was turned into a hospital room, and another private duty nurse was hired to take care of Bettsie's medical needs, therapy, and special diet.

At Hopkins for a check-up after two months of chemotherapy, her surgeon found new cancer cells. Bettsie had been losing weight, had difficulty breathing, and was unable to walk without support. Sholom was at her side day and night, but after four months of suffering, Bettsie passed away.

The funeral home was full to the last seat. Representatives of the Associated Endowment Fund, of HIAS, of Hadassah, the Smorodna compatriots, the National Committee of Labor Israel, *Histadrut,* all the members of the Baltimore Committee of New Americans, the organization of Holocaust survivors, the Rotstein Family Circle, and many employees of the Levinson Furniture Factory all came to pay their respects and pass by the plain, black-draped coffin.

After short eulogies by Rabbis Nathan Drazin, Dr.

Samuel Rosenblatt, and Elimelech Hertzberg, the coffin was rolled out and taken to the cemetery in Randallstown. Oscar and Frumele brought the traditional after-funeral meal, hard-cooked eggs and dark bread, to the *Shiva* home (house of mourning). Throughout the seven days of mourning, Sholom's home was full of people who came to pay their condolences and attend morning and evening prayers.

At the end of the *Shiva* week, Sholom gathered his daughters and son in the living room and asked them to decide if they wanted to take over the running of the factory, or would they rather that Sholom sell it. "I'm exhausted, and at a total loss now, without your mother," he stammered, as he broke into tears. "All these years, I've been preoccupied with the factory and community activities, and all the family things we had planned for. . . . Time just passed her by. So much remains unfulfilled."

"What are you going to do?"

"I don't know yet. I need to get away from the factory. Maybe I'll go to Israel, to see our *landsleit* from Smorodna."

♦ ♦ ♦

My dear Jacob and Emily,

It is a month today since we lost Bettsie. I still can't find a moment to calm my pain. Every night I lie awake, waiting for her to crawl into my arms. I keep thinking that this is just a bad dream, that she is just on vacation and will be back soon. All her things are still here, and I imagine her coming home, opening the door to our room, and asking if I'm asleep already.

I'm writing this, not to cry on your shoulders, for the hurt and the loss are yours just as they are ours. I grieve for

Bettsie, and cry myself to sleep every night.

They rented (tore) my garment at her funeral and rented my heart forever.

I am writing to let you know that today we met with the attorneys and the real estate people, and signed an agreement leasing the factory and sub-leasing the warehouse to the new owners. The Levinson Furniture Factory was an exciting business. It became a frightening place after the riots, erupting daily in arguments, racial conflicts, merciless competition and lack of discipline by our workers. Even the union is helpless. Workers come and go, or don't come at all. There is chaos in the factory, and stealing at the warehouse.

Jimmie was doing a good job; I was very proud of him, but some of the younger workers are paying little attention to him. He is too young and too white to give them orders. He decided that he wants to finish law school. Eve plans to go to Israel, to the Technion, for a degree in architecture. She is already a good designer, and is fluent in Hebrew. Lorna will graduate from Loyola College this spring, and is working as a substitute teacher in the Baltimore County schools. There is no glamour in teaching here, but it's even more dangerous teaching in downtown Baltimore. She likes it and is not a bit frightened.

So, my dear Jacob and Emily, it was a unanimous family decision that we sell the business. I appreciate all your help and your confidence in me, entrusting me with your factory but I am more thankful to you for entrusting me with your daughter. I can't continue building furniture; my whole world has collapsed.

Jimmie and I will help the new owners for a reasonable period of time, and then I will take a rest, visiting Eve at the Technion and travelling around Israel, seeing my Smorodna

landsleit. I also want to donate a room in the new Hadassah
Hospital in Jerusalem in Bettsie's memory. May she rest in
peace. The children send their love.

    Zait Gezund! [Stay well.]
      Sol

♦ ♦ ♦

I. Bettsie
A delicate face, but skin and bones,
A look which glowed like candle fire,
Gentle, soft voice in dying tones,
Yet refusing to give up, to expire.

To the very last she was vital, active,
Dictated letters, demanded, inspired,
Concealing her suffering, in pain reflective,
She called her parents, cajoled, inquired.
And now the light is out, extinguished.
Of a child-like face and delicate form;
She was strong, effective, distinguished,
A fine person, a shield against the storm.

II
You gazed intensely at me. "Come nearer,"
you said, and tried hard to smile;
but the pain was too deep, your breath
almost gone, too weak to utter more words.

You were remarkably pleasant and calm,
but your eyes showed the pangs and cramps

your body experienced in our presence,
covering up the sufferings with a smile.

You went through life proud of your past,
accepting your fate and unshakenly walked
with it, despite all obstacles, temptations;
now comes the end, your voice - a dying breath.

Only two words your lips uttered: "Be Well".
You smiled and closed your sunken eyes;
I said: "Speedy Recovery". You mumbled: "Too late".
I kissed your cold, bony hand and I left. . . .

in sorrow, Frumele

26

HANS ALFRED VON GISMARK was a descendant of an old Prussian and Pomeranian family. He belonged to the so-called higher class of Germans, not particularly interested in politics, but ultra-nationalists just the same. Hans was a landowner and industrialist, with forest holdings in Pomerania, Prussia, Eastern Poland, and South America.

When he was seventeen, his family moved to Brazil, and he attended Sao Paulo University, where he learned Portuguese, Spanish and English. After his mother suffered a stroke, the whole family, except for his sister Gertrude, returned to Germany. Gertrude decided to continue her studies, first in Brazil, and then in Argentina.

Hans was called to military service because of his knowledge of languages and his family background. Sent to the Military Intelligence School in Frankfurt, he was highly respected by the official Nazi leadership and the *Wehrmacht* Command. In the spring of 1938, his father died, and Hans took over his father's business holdings in Poland, and became involved with the upper strata of the Polish government. He joined Polish Foreign Minister Beck, General Rydz-Smigly, and other leaders of the Polish government in hunting expeditions attended by Hermann Goering and other high functionaries of the Nazi party.

A year after their father died, Gertrude came from Rio for a visit, but the Nazi environment, the parades, and demonstrations spoiled her stay in Germany, and she returned to Brazil.

In June, 1939, Hans was called back for military duty in the Gestapo Special Intelligence Service Unit. His father's support for the Nazis, his Iron Cross medal of World War I, other decorations, and his own knowledge of languages made Hans a most valuable asset to the *Gestapo* and the *Wehrmacht.* He was one of the first officers to arrive in the war zone when the German armies occupied Eastern Poland.

He witnessed the round up of Jews who were herded into former Polish army barracks to repair them after the destruction caused by the *Messerschmidt* bombings. He witnessed the selections of Jews who were then shipped to the forests to be shot. Only a handful of Jews, those who worked in the military barracks, temporarily survived the selections. Some managed to escape, crossing the borders to White Russia and to Lithuania.

While not occupied with his work translating Polish Army documents and interrogating former Polish government functionaries, Hans walked the streets of Smorodna, observing the horrid, daily violence against the remnants of the Jewish community, the beatings and the random shootings. He experienced some doubts, pangs of conscience and inner conflicts with the policies of the occupation armies. The more he saw, the more frustrated he became, and the more he turned to his work, translating seized documents.

He avoided the public hangings and shootings of people who had tried to escape, or were found hiding during mass selections.

He spent his evenings in his little house at *Gestapo* headquarters, drinking, listening to news broadcasts from Berlin, and worrying about his sick, wheelchair-bound mother. He knew that the nurse who attended his mother, *Fraulein* Verda, was old, forgetful, and half blind. The other household help were trained to cook and clean, but not to care for an eighty-year-old invalid.

One evening, after another heavy bout of drinking, he asked for a transfer to Berlin, which was closer to home. He thought that perhaps his knowledge of languages would land him an assignment in a Latin American country. Perhaps he could get a doctor's opinion that his mother needed a warmer climate, and he would be allowed to accompany her to Brazil, where Gertrude lived. Once in Brazil there would be no going back to Hitler's Germany.

The next morning, he found Smorodna's streets becoming more and more deserted, except for the two blocks surrounded by Lithuanian guards and barbed wire, where young Jews, employed by the military, still lived. The rest of the town's houses were already occupied by Germans or Poles, or had been taken apart by peasant-hooligans who roamed the streets, taking everything they could from the empty houses.

Hans knew that even the remaining Jews, the young who were still capable of working, were doomed to be liquidated. He went to the *Gestapo* offices and asked for a three-day pass to Plathe to visit his mother, and requested permission to take a Polish maid with him to work as a housekeeper for his mother.

The Jewish girls who cleaned rooms and houses for the German officers lived in those two remaining streets of Smorodna. After they had finished cleaning, they would receive a half loaf of bread, some margarine and jam and, sometimes, a few potatoes or beets, before they were marched home, under guard, to be picked up for work the next morning.

The girl who was assigned to clean Hans' little house was Chanele. At first she was terrified of the often-drunk officer who looked at her with lusting eyes. One day he asked if she spoke German. She answered, more in Yiddish than in German, *"A bischien* (a little)."

"Do you know how to cook?"

"A bischien."

"Are you healthy?"

"Until now, thank God, yes."

"Did you go to school here?"

"Yes, last year I graduated from the *Gymnasium.*"

"Would you like to clean house and take care of an elderly woman on an estate in Germany?"

"My parents are here. They were taken away in a selection last week. I hope to find them soon."

"Sorry, but all Jews and Poles will be removed from this area to make room for more military units to be stationed here. None of the Jews resettled to other places will ever return here. Think fast. I'm leaving tonight for a short visit to my mother. Finish cleaning, and give me your name, age, and place of birth. What is your name?"

"Chana."

"No good. We'll change it to Halina, and we'll change your family name and religion, too. I'll write in your travel documents that your nationality is *Folks-Deutsche,* and that you registered of your own free will to work as a maid in Pomerania. Think fast. Maybe I'm half-crazy, but maybe it will work. You have nothing to lose. I know what fate awaits your people here. Perhaps I can save you. When you finish cleaning, stay in the house, in the dark, until I return."

He dressed in his uniform, took a bag full of imported delicatessen meats, and several bottles of wine, and left. Chanele was full of fear and despair. Her heart pounded wildly, and she was short of breath. What should she do? Run away? But to where? Guards were stationed outside the houses. She sat in the dark house and listened as guards walked past. She wondered what she was doing, abandoning her parents, abandoning Sholom. It was conceivable that Hans would take her somewhere, hurt her, and dispose of her. God only knows what will happen.

When Hans returned he still smelled of wine. Holding a bundle of clothes and a small wooden suitcase, he handed Chanele some documents. "These are your new identification cards, a *Ken-Karte*. Read them and try to remember your new name, family name, and place of birth. When we reach *Schneidermuhl*, border inspectors will board the train and ask for your documents. Answer only if they ask you questions. Let me do the talking."

Late that evening, dressed in new peasant clothes, they left the house in a military jeep for the railroad station. The driver, a corporal, and Hans smoked, drank, laughed, and joked all the way to the station. They travelled for hours on a military train with mostly men, and only a few women passengers, nurses in military uniforms, and a few civilian women. No one paid any attention to the peasant girl.

The train stopped at the border, and the inspectors were swift, but polite. They saluted Hans with *Heil Hitler!* and hardly looked at her documents. Two hours later they arrived at the train station at Plathe.

A carriage was waiting for them in the darkness. Chanele was frightened, but curious. They drove through the huge gates of a palace, and she was taken to an attic room by an elderly woman. "Halina, this is your room. Before you go to sleep, take a shower down the hall. We will talk in the morning. Don't unpack your things; we'll give you our own clothes."

The elderly woman left the room and returned with a glass of milk and a piece of bread, but Chanele wasn't able to eat. After showering, she went to her room and fell asleep.

27

THE ESTATE BELONGED TO Hans Alfred Von Gismark and his widowed mother. Chanele, now Halina, quickly learned to speak German and to care for *Frau* Gismark. Her anxiety and fear gradually disappeared, for she was no longer a victim or a martyr.

There were only a few people working at the estate, most of them elderly; most of the young ones were in the military. The elderly woman, *Fraulein* Verda, was half blind, a very religious person, who was always praying, meditating, or talking to herself. She was reasonable with Halina, but very strict about following doctor's orders and all of Hans' instructions after he returned to his army post. Otherwise, she was friendly and humane, asking Halina about her family and why she didn't receive any letters from home. Halina told her that her mother had died and her father had remarried, that his second wife was very cruel to her.

"I never married," *Fraulein* Verda told her. "I will be like a mother to you." Halina burst into tears, and *Fraulein* Verda never mentioned the subject again.

On Christmas eve, after returning from the family chapel where they held midnight Mass, Halina found Christmas gifts from *Frau* Gismark, *Fraulein* Verda, and a card from Hans, with a thank you note "for taking good care of my mother."

That spring, more women came to work on the estate, in the mansion, in the garden, and in the manor house. Both men and women worked in the fields and cleaned the walkways. Some elderly men were trained as gardeners who worked for Hans at his forests in eastern Poland and came, not as slave laborers, but as volunteers, to work on the Gismark manor. Halina stayed out of their way, afraid to be discovered or recognized by the Polish workers. After the daily chores she did for *Frau* Gismark, she would go to her room, listen to her *Telefunken* radio and read about the "resettlement of the Jews from Poland to work camps," the struggle against epidemics in the areas of German administration, and the establishment of camps for skilled Jewish workers.

Life on the estate was normal compared with the rest of the towns in Pomerania. There were no shortages in the kitchen and no lack of medications for *Frau* Gismark. Packages arrived regularly from Hans in Poland, and medications arrived from Gertrude in Brazil through the International Red Cross. A Doctor Arndt from Labes came almost every week to examine *Frau* Gismark. He gave her injections and left instructions for Halina.

In January of 1944, Hans Alfred Von Gismark returned home by ambulance on a stretcher. One of his arms was in a sling, and one of his legs was amputated. He had been on a train from Vilno to Grodno, when partisans in Vilno derailed the train, which was also carrying several hundred Italian and German soldiers returning from the Russian front. Hundreds were killed, and hundreds more wounded.

When the guards opened fire on the partisans, they blew up the train and Hans was among the wounded.

He was taken to the Neugard Military Hospital, where his severely injured leg was amputated. At his personal request, he was sent home to his estate, only a short ride from Neugard. Compassion overwhelmed Halina when Hans was carried to his room, and she cried like a child. It came upon her so naturally, so strongly, and she could not compose herself. She knew that he was an SS officer; she had seen framed pictures of Hermann Goering and Hitler over his desk. She also knew that he had saved her life.

A military nurse came from Neugard and offered to stay at the estate to help Hans with the therapy that he needed. He thanked her for the offer but insisted, instead, that she teach Halina how to undress him, change his dressings, and sponge and wash him. At first Halina was embarrassed when she had to do these things, but she grew to trust him.

She knew Hans was telling her the truth about what happened to the Jewish people of the Soviet Union, Poland, the Baltic countries, Czechoslovakia, and the other countries which were occupied by Germany.

"Smorodna weighs heavily on my conscience. We lost this war both militarily and morally," he said sadly. "Madness still runs our country. I hope this suicidal insanity will end soon and you will be able to return home."

"Home? After all you've told me? I don't have a home anymore!"

"Halina, if you want to, you can stay here. I will take care of you as you have taken care of my mother."

"We live on borrowed time, and who knows what will happen tomorrow? One thing is certain, I will not go back to Smorodna. Time healed nothing and we are still trapped in this war. The most important thing now is for you to get better."

♦ ♦ ♦

Halina worked on the estate until the Soviet Army came to Plathe in March, 1945. Old *Fraulein* Verda was sick with an asthmatic condition, so Dr. Arndt was called from Labes. He took her to his newly organized hospital for civilians when the Russian *Commandantura* ordered all residents out of the estate, and Halina took *Frau* Gismark to a vacant house in Plathe whose owners had escaped when the Russians came close to the town. Halina went to the *Commandantura* and told them that this elderly woman had saved her life. She was promised food allocations for herself and *Frau* Gismark.

Dr. Arndt, she discovered, was a Jewish doctor who had been hidden all the years of the Nazi regime by his Christian wife and supported by some German friends, including *Frau* Verda and Hans.

Hans was in Halle-Mersenburg when the Russians occupied Plathe. He was there to be fitted with an artificial leg. A Jewish officer in the Polish medical unit stationed in Plathe offered Halina a job as nurse and translator in the small local hospital and repatriation station (PUR), but she refused.

In June, 1945, orders were issued that all Germans must evacuate Pomerania and return to Germany, but Dr. Arndt was permitted to remain. Halina decided to leave with *Frau* Gismark for Stettin. From there they crossed the Oder River to Frankfurt/Am Osten. Halina was able to find Hans in a prisoner-of-war hospital in Halle-Mersenburg, awaiting sentencing as a Nazi war criminal.

When she went to see him, he was pale and ill, but in good spirits. He was happy to see his mother in her wheelchair, still alive. Halina went to the Russian *Commandantura* in Halle and signed sworn statements that Hans Gismark had saved her life; that he was not a murderer, but one who hated the Nazi regime.

A week later, Hans came to them. They spent the rest of the day just talking. That night, Halina offered him her bed, helped him remove his artificial leg, and then she went to sleep on the old sofa. In the middle of the night, she heard him moaning and went to check on him. As she sat at the edge of the bed, he took her hand in his and told her how much he appreciated all that she had done for his mother and him.

And Halina thanked him for saving her life. "Apparently we both did what was right and God saved us."

"Halina, I'm planning to leave Europe. Some Germans are still talking about revenge. They didn't learn anything from this terrible tragedy we brought to our country, to Europe, and to humanity."

"Where do you want to go?"

"To Brazil. My sister, Gertrude, lives in Rio de Janeiro. We have some land holdings there and some financial interests that can help me live comfortably with my mother for the rest of our lives."

"Why are you telling me this?"

"I'd like you to join us."

"Don't you think that I should return to Poland, to see if any of my family or friends survived?"

As gently as he could, he told Halina that they had all perished in Treblinka, Sobibor, and Majdanek. "There has

not been one Jew in Smorodna since 1942. Unless one of
them escaped to the Soviet Union, survived, and then returned, there are no Jews left in your town. Halina, I'm
making you an offer, just as I did that night in Smorodna
in 1939. Come with us, and marry me. My mother already
calls you her daughter; she loves you as I do. I know this is
awkward, but I have admired you from the moment I met
you in my home in Smorodna. Together, let's build a future
away from here, away from all the hatred and racial mis-
trust. I will make it up to you for all these years of darkness
and suffering."

"No one can make up for all that I have lost, my
parents, my boyfriend, my youth."

"I know this, and I understand. Still, please consider
what I've said. Let's talk about it some more in the morning. May I kiss you goodnight?" Halina didn't answer him,
just bent over and kissed his unshaven cheek.

♦ ♦ ♦

In December, 1947, Halina married Hans Alfred Von
Gismark and they left for Rio.

They bought a comfortable home in a quiet neighborhood, had a maid, a cook, and a gardener, as well as a
driver for a specially-equipped van for *Frau* Gismark. They
went to the beach daily, and Halina learned Spanish and
Portuguese. It was a very comfortable life.

Most of their neighbors were absolutely wonderful. They
were the elite of Rio, bankers, industrialists, college profes-
sors, and writers. Many proudly announced that they were
Marranos, the descendants of the early Jews, people who
had left Portugal in the sixteenth century to escape the
Inquisition.

Hans changed his name to Henrico. He felt it was necessary for his business, and didn't want to be asked if he were related to the famous German family Gismark. He travelled often to Uruguay and Argentina, and frequently received invitations to conferences of former Nazi officers living in South America. He always turned them down, claiming that his health situation would not allow it, and that his war wounds limited his social activities.

In 1950, Halina gave birth to twin girls. She named one after her mother, Esther, and the other after Wilhemina Gismark, who had passed away in Halina's arms in June of that year.

In 1965, Henrico, Halina, Esther, and Wilma visited Switzerland, Italy and France together. Then, while Henrico went to Germany, Halina, with his approval, went to Israel.

The girls knew that they were Jewish, and they had Jewish friends in school, although they didn't observe any Jewish customs or traditions.

The visit to Israel opened a floodgate of memories for Halina, and a longing for her past. They travelled the small country from Tel Chai to Eilat, the cities and open spaces, the valleys and hills. They photographed the Carmel, monuments, mountains, and parks. And finally they visited Yad Vashem. Halina wept silently as she searched for the names of relatives. Her parents were listed among the *kedoshim,* the martyrs of Smorodna killed in the first action, in the forest outside the town, by the *Einsatztruppen.* She looked for the family of Sholom Schwartzman, but no one was listed among the martyrs.

In Haifa, she found a family from Smorodna. Halina called them, and they invited her to their home. When their hostess looked at Esther and Wilma, with their light hair and blue eyes, she asked if Halina's husband was Jewish. Halina's response, that he was not, but that he had saved her life during the war, brought an icy stare and a look of scorn.

Halina felt that her visit here was a waste, and that she was not welcome. They left without having found any more information on other survivors from Smorodna. She and the girls met Henrico in Zurich, and they all returned to Rio.

Henrico swore that never again would he go to Germany, and Halina decided that never again would she go to Israel.

28

THE NEW OWNERS of the Levinson Furniture Factory were owners of a chain of stores. Everything the factory produced was sold in their stores' furniture departments. The success of the products the factory produced was astonishing. Sales were unbelievable, and they were forced to add another shift and hire more employees. They transferred Joseph Klein, one of their store managers, to the factory to supervise the increased production. Orders exceeded their wildest expectations, and Sholom, who was only supposed to come in three days a week to consult, came in every day instead. He and Joseph planned new styles of sofas, chairs, cabinets, end tables, fancy display cases, cherry beds, and rosewood dining room sets.

Joseph Klein was the son of Pinchas Klein, Baltimore community leader and benefactor of the local Talmud Torah and Talmudical Academy. Joseph and Sholom took a liking to each other from the moment they met. Both were interested in Jewish education. Joseph himself was active at the Board of Jewish Education and the Baltimore Hebrew College, under the leadership of the prominent scholar and educator, Dr. Louis L. Kaplan. Sholom served on the board of HIAS of Baltimore. Both were friends and admirers of

Harry Greenstein, the director of the Associated Jewish Charities.

Harry had served in Europe as director of UNRRA, and had helped liquidate the D.P. camps in Austria and Germany. He had been an advisor to General Lucius D. Clay, Commander-in-Chief of the United States Forces in Europe, and advisor on Jewish affairs to John J. McCloy, first United States High Commissioner to West Germany.

Harry shared with Joseph and Sholom stories from his trips to Dachau, Warsaw, Vienna, and Berlin, moving and interesting tales about the survivors and the camps.

When Joseph worked with Sholom on a daily basis, a close friendship developed between the two men. Even after full days of hard work, they still found time to share their thoughts about Judaism, their children, and education. They both agreed with the view that only a meaningful, higher Jewish education could save the younger generation from assimilation, and that education in general is the key to most good things America has to offer her youth.

Although it took only a few weeks for Joseph to learn all the secrets of the manufacturing trade, all there was to know about production and management/worker relations, he insisted that Sholom and Jimmie live up to the letter of the sales agreement, and continue to consult with the new management on how to run the factory.

One day at lunch Sholom turned to Joseph, "We agreed to come in to help three days a week, four hours a day, but now I'm working full time, much harder than I worked for myself, and I need a rest. You know enough to run this factory, and Jimmie is willing to stay on until next semester. I'd like to travel, to Israel or the Orient, just to get away for a while."

"I can't make this decision alone, without asking the board of directors, but I have another solution to your problem. How about a vacation at our expense? The furniture section of our store is sending buyers to Argentina and Brazil to select and purchase leather furniture. We'll pay your travel expenses, put you up in the best hotels, and give you a *per diem*. The companies we deal with will wine and dine you, so instead of my going, I'll suggest that they send you. I'll miss you, as our advisor and as my friend, but this will do you good. So, say that you'll do it and I'll try to arrange it."

Three weeks later, Sholom was on his way to the South American Republic of Brazil, to the cities of Rio de Janeiro and Sao Paulo. He left Baltimore at six o'clock in the evening for New York, and from there, south on VARIG Airlines, on which he slept soundly. When he awoke, he was already in Rio. After passport control, he entered the spacious Rio terminal, where a young woman was waiting for him, holding a card with his name. She introduced herself in correct English, "My name is Wilma. Welcome to Brazil, Mr. Schwartzman. We are happy to have you here. The Sheraton is only a short walk from our office, and our chauffeur, Pedro, will be at your service while you're in Rio. I should tell you that the beach is very close to your hotel."

"Thank you, Wilma. I want to visit the factories first, and swimming will have to come later. Right now, I'd like to go to my hotel, freshen up, and change clothes. It's winter in Baltimore, and here it's hot."

Pedro took his suitcases as Wilma introduced him. "Pedro speaks English, German, Spanish, and Portuguese. He was born in Portugal, and served in Africa during the war. He was a prisoner of war in Italy. Just tell him when

and where to pick you up, and he'll take you wherever you
want to go. I have to go back to the office. Here's our card;
call if you need anything, and we'll see you tomorrow at
nine o'clock at the office."

Pedro drove the station wagon to the Sheraton, handed
Sholom's suitcases to the doorman, and left. Sholom un-
packed, then sent a telegram to Joseph Klein:

*"Just arrived. No problems. Good service. Good reception. Good
room. Mild weather. Say Hi to Jimmie. Sol."*

The next morning, Sholom climbed out of bed early,
ecstatic when he saw the sun shining over Rio, in contrast
to the rain and snow just two days ago in New York.
Savoring the pleasure of the morning air for the first time
in a long time, he hummed a song while he dressed in a
light summer suit.

Apparently, people here dress informally, without ties,
and he even noticed in the hotel cafeteria that men were
wearing shorts. The buffet had a wide assortment of cheeses,
pastries, fish, eggs, and fruit. He had pancakes and a cup of
coffee, and after breakfast called Pedro. By the time he got
his briefcase and came back downstairs, the chauffeur was
waiting for him.

It was only a short ride to the one-story building with
the sign in Portuguese, "Henrico Gismark Industries, Inc."
Inside, a reception room was decorated with photos of furniture and household goods and posters of international
furniture exhibits and shows.

A young woman greeted him with a friendly, "Good
morning, Mr. Schwartzman. How are you?"

"Good morning, Miss Wilma, it's nice to see you again."

"I'm not Wilma, I'm Esther. We're twins and everyone makes this mistake. Did you get some rest?"

"Yes, I did. Thanks."

"Can I offer you some coffee, juice, or a cold drink?"

"I'd like some cold water please."

They walked into a dark-panelled office furnished with desks of Brazilian wood, a heavy bookcase, and a wheel-chair. On the leather-covered desk next to the telephone, Sholom noticed a picture of a woman with the twin girls. All three women had blond hair, and were sitting by a pool in swim suits.

The woman in that picture so much reminded him of someone in his life from long ago, Chanele. But the Chanele he remembered had dark hair, and besides, what's the use of comparing pictures to someone who had gone so long ago?

His thoughts were interrupted when a man wheeled himself into the office. "Good morning, Mr. Schwartzman. Welcome. I'm Henrico Gismark. Sorry I kept you waiting. How was your trip?"

"VARIG Airlines is wonderful. Everyone is so polite."

"We are known for our courtesy in Brazil. I've gotten together a collection of our catalogues showing all our latest creations. Take your time and see if there's anything here that you would like. If you find something that interests you, my daughter will take you to our showrooms."

Sholom opened the first catalogue and was impressed with the unique and innovatively designed leather otto-mans and chairs. Esther returned with a plate of fruit and more water. While Sholom studied the other catalogues, Henrico answered telephone calls, made some notes, and signed papers at his desk. Esther took the papers and was about to leave the office when her father asked her to take

Mr. Schwartzman to the showroom. "If there's anything he wants to order from the catalogue that we don't have in stock at the moment, we can order it for him."

"I'm ready to go whenever you are."

"Then let's go."

Sholom liked the assortment of elegant, distinctly designed Brazilian furniture, leather sofas, and Brazilian wood wall systems. When they returned from the showroom, Sholom handed Henrico a marked catalogue with a substantial order.

"Very impressive. Thank you. You must have a giant operation in Baltimore."

"Yes, we do. We have six large department stores."

"We'll start working on your order immediately. I know you have more business to attend to while you're here, but would you like to have dinner with us this afternoon? We have our dinners when you in the States eat lunch."

"I have an appointment in a linoleum factory at eleven o'clock, and I don't know how long it will take, but I hope to be done about one. Would that be convenient for you?"

"It's just right. Pedro can drive you to the linoleum factory and wait for you, take you back to your hotel, if you like, and then bring you to our home. Thank you again for your order, and we'll look forward to seeing you later."

Henrico wheeled himself out of his office, leaving Esther and Sholom to sign the order forms. Esther called Pedro, and then asked Sholom if she could ride with him to the linoleum factory because she had some questions she wanted to ask him.

"Mr. Schwartzman, how do they treat *mischlinge* (children of mixed marriages) in Israel? My father is German and my mother is Jewish. He saved her life during the war, and they married after the war. Neither of them belongs to any religious community. We have friends who are children of mixed marriages, and, with very few exceptions, they have all joined Christian churches. Both my sister and I, however, would like to marry Jewish men and lead full Jewish lives. We want to belong somewhere. I dream of going to America or to Israel. We're looking for an identity, but who are we? It's not enough to be called Brazilians; we're searching for our roots.

"My father was ostracized from his roots. He's German, you know, and our mother was condemned by her people for marrying a German. And even in Brazil, the local Germans look down on my father for having married a Slavic woman. Even the parents of our Jewish friends at school object to their children's friendships with us. They never let them sleep over at our home. Do you think there's a way to get to America to start a new life? Could we get in on student visas?"

"Perhaps, but will your parents let you go?"

"Our father is a very sick man. He's got kidney problems in addition to having had his leg amputated, and the doctors here can't help him. He's gone to Switzerland and Sweden, but the doctors there haven't been able to help him either. We've been staying here because of our parents and the business, although we really don't need the business. Father sold his land interests in Europe and has enough to live on without the business, but money isn't everything. We want our own life, and we want to be happy. We love our parents, and they love us, but we want our own nests, our own little corner on this globe.

"For all our lives, our father has been sick, and our

mother has taken care of him. She is his nurse, his maid, and his servant, and she worships him because he saved her life. She's strong, and she can take it, but we're young, and we want something more. We want to have a good time like our friends. We never go anywhere; we're always the factory representatives dealing with the buyers and salesmen. Some of them are fresh."

"Why do you invite them to your home?"

"It's the custom here, to invite guests from overseas to your home."

"Can I still change my mind, and say I can't make it?"

"Oh, please don't. We really want you to come."

"All right. Pedro can pick me up at 12:45."

He stayed for just a short while at the linoleum factory. He didn't like the designs, and the merchandise was too expensive compared with Mexican products, so he went back to the hotel, changed clothes, bought a bottle of wine and some flowers, and by 12:45 Pedro was waiting for him.

The villa was surrounded by stately palms, lots of wild flowers, and a lovely iron gate.

The girls, dressed in shorts, greeted Sholom warmly. Henrico wheeled onto the front porch. "Welcome to our home, Mr. Schwartzman. Please, have a seat. Would you like something cold to drink? My wife, Halina, will be out in a minute. Your name sounds German."

"No, I'm Jewish, and I'm from Poland."

"So are my wife and children. We can talk more during dinner. Let's go eat."

They all followed Henrico to a large dining room. Sholom sat between Wilma and Esther, and Henrico at the head of the table. A tall, blond woman came in from the kitchen.

"Excuse me, we're short of help today. I'm Halina."

Sholom stood up and put out his hand to greet her. "I'm Sol Schwartzman."

Halina turned pale, grabbed her chest, and fainted. Wilma caught her mother, and Esther quickly got some water from the kitchen. When Halina came to, Henrico asked her what had happened, but Halina passed it off with, "Nothing, Henrico, I'm fine. I feel better now, let's sit down and eat," which they did, in total silence.

No one knew what had happened, and everyone was worried about her. After dinner Henrico excused himself. He needed to rest, doctor's orders, and he said goodbye to Sholom. "It was so nice to meet you, and we're delighted to be doing business with you. We'll ship your order as soon as it's ready, and you have a safe trip home."

Wilma and Esther helped the maid clear the table, while Halina sat on the porch with a glass of water. Sholom turned to say goodbye. "I'm sorry, Mrs. Gismark, if I caused you any trouble. It was nice to meet you. I had looked forward to talking to you — your daughters told me that you are Jewish, but I can see that you're not feeling well. Perhaps another time we'll be able to talk."

Halina started to weep, "Sholom! *Du Derkenst mich Nisht? Dos Bin Ich. . . . Chana Goratski, Chanele.* Sholom, don't you recognize me? It's me, Chanele, from Smorodna!"

This time Sholom thought that HE would pass out. His voice was but a whisper, "Chanele? I didn't recognize you! Your hair, your voice, the make-up, the years — everything's changed. I looked for you all over the world, in every newspaper I could find, at Yad Vashem and through the Red Cross. I couldn't find you!"

Esther and Wilma came running from the kitchen,

"Mama, what happened? Is Mr. Schwartzman alright?"

"Mr. Schwartzman and I came from the same town in Poland. We grew up together and fell in love. We were going to get married and go to Palestine, but the war separated us and now, after thirty years, he is a guest in our home! What a small world! What a miracle!" Halina couldn't stop crying.

"Sholom, tell me what your life has been like. Are you married? Do you have children? Do you know if any of our compatriots survived?"

Sholom told Chanele about Bettsie and his children, and about the Smorodna compatriots living in Baltimore. Chanele talked about the *landsmen* living in Sao Paulo.

"They don't speak to me; they consider me an *oysvorf* (outcast). They say that I betrayed the memory of my parents by marrying a German, but they don't understand. He risked his life to save me from Treblinka. Please, Sholom, don't judge me too harshly. I am the same Chanele you left in Smorodna. When I came home the second night from the *kazarmes* (barracks), my home was already occupied by the Germans, and I couldn't find my parents. I saw what happened when they set fire to the *Beis Midrash*. I had nothing left to live for — even you were gone. On the spur of the moment, Henrico offered me a job to take care of his mother, and that job saved my life. After the war, I married him because he was a good man. He is a good husband and a good father. Nationality? Religion? I don't care. Where was God when our *Beis Midrash* was burning, with all the women and children, and all those elderly pious Jews, locked inside?"

Sholom fought back his tears. "I'm not judging you, Chanele. I'm just so glad that you survived." He sat with

Chanele and her children for a long time, until he realized that his plane was due to leave very soon for Sao Paulo.

"I'd love to stay longer. I'll call you. Here is my address. Please write to me, and I'll definitely write back. And you, Esther and Wilma, take good care of your parents. I promise to stay in touch. It really hurts to leave now, but I must."

When he returned to his hotel, there was an urgent message waiting for him to call home. Jimmie answered, "Daddy, I have some bad news. Oscar Glazman passed away. Please come home. Frumele is in bad shape."

29

SHOLOM WENT DIRECTLY to the airport, paid the difference for changing his return ticket, and after waiting at Sao Paulo for two hours, caught a flight to Miami, and the connection to Baltimore. He arrived, exhausted, and took a cab directly to Frumele's home. The *Shiva* house was full of people who had come for the evening service.

Sholom greeted his Smorodna *landsmen,* members of the Rotstein Family Circle, and Rabbi Herzberg. Frumele was sitting in a low chair, dressed in black. She welcomed Sholom with a sad smile and, holding back her tears, told him that the doctor said it was hypertension. "He had a heart attack, and by the time the ambulance arrived, he was gone."

Between *Mincha* and *Maariv* services, Rabbi Herzberg spoke, "I knew Oscar, *olov-hasholom,* for all my years in Baltimore. I'd like to tell Frumele, Jacob, and Bernie that your influence on him, your love, and dedication, saved his life after his great tragedy. He told me that you, Frumele, didn't have a religious upbringing but that Divine goodness flows through your veins. He told me this while you were in Israel, and how grateful he was for all the years of joy and happiness you shared. He also had doubts, for when his terrible misfortune happened, he felt that his life had been destroyed, but meeting you, Frumele, and having Jacob and Bernie, brought new hope to his heart. You inspired him, and he returned to his faith.

"God works in mysterious ways. We never know who, as God's messenger, will bring back children to the fold of their parents, or parents to the fold of their people. If you find it difficult to pray, come to the synagogue to meditate, to say *Kaddish*. Oscar deserves to be remembered.

"I will remember him as a *mensch* with a conscience of a saint. Be content that Oscar's soul is now in Heaven with his loved ones.

"As we said this morning, 'The Lord redeemeth the souls of His servants, and none of them that trust in Him shall be forsaken.'

"May Oscar's soul be bound up in the bond of life eternal, and grant that the memory of Oscar's life inspire us all to noble and consecrated living. Amen."

◆ ◆ ◆

Some people helped themselves to coffee and plain cakes after *Maariv* service, and then most of them left. Some friends of the children sat in the kitchen, talking about the Orioles. Sholom sat down in a low chair next to Frumele, and covered her hand with his. "I'm sorry I wasn't here for the funeral. I was in Brazil."

"I know, Jimmie told me. He was a great help to the boys and me, making funeral arrangements. He was here this morning, before going to the factory."

"I haven't been home yet. I came here straight from the airport."

Sholom sat for a while, listening to Frumele talk about

Oscar, and about the many people who came to the funeral. Then she asked him about his trip, and if he'd met any compatriots from Smorodna.

"Yes, I found Chanele Goratski, my old girlfriend. She's married and has two daughters."

"Why weren't you able to find her all these years?"

"She married a rich German, changed her name, changed the color of her hair, and moved to Brazil."

"One of ours married a German? What kind of person is she?"

"Don't judge her. He risked his life to save hers. I met him, and he's a good person, a *leitisher mensch* (decent human being)."

"Are you going to keep in touch with her?"

"Yes, of course. With her and her two daughters. They are looking for roots — they want to be Jewish. They want to come to America, or go to Israel, and start a new life. They live there like the Marranos lived in Brazil for hundreds of years."

"Why didn't they join a local synagogue or an organization of survivors? There are 50,000 Jews living in Brazil. They couldn't find themselves a place to live as Jews?"

"They are condemned and ostracized by their fellow Jews, especially by her fellow survivors, because she married a German. He's from a family of famous Prussian *Junkers.*"

"It's tragic. What will you do?"

"I'm going to help the two girls emigrate to Israel, or come here. They're our compatriots, too, aren't they?"

30

Dear Frumele,

I've just returned from South America. The magic of Brazil and Argentina were good for my spirits. I went to Sao Paulo, as I promised Mr. Klein, and ordered an entire line of the finest furniture and fabrics available. They've got reclining chairs with a new twist, originality, and low price that should do wonders for our profits, and pay for my trips to Buzios, Ignassu and Falls Salvador.

I didn't go to Rio. I just couldn't face Chanele again. I spoke to her twice on the phone, and also to Esther and Mr. Gismark. Chanele told him everything about us. He kept saying how sorry he is for what happened in Smorodna and to European Jewry. He gave me his word of honor that he, himself, never killed any Jews, anyone, during the war. He invited me to come and visit, and told me that their home was mine, and they'd all like to see me again, but I politely declined his invitation, saying that my travels in Brazil and Argentina are strictly business, and that my time is limited.

In Sao Paulo I met Elkana Charmatz, the co-editor of

191

the Yiddish paper, Novo Momento. *He is a poet and a writer from Sosnowitz, Poland, and a survivor of Auschwitz-Birkenau. He told me that when he was the editor of the* Yiddish Presse *in Rio he interviewed Halina Gismark about her experiences during the first days of the Nazi occupation of Smorodna.*

Her husband declined to be interviewed. He also told me that the Gismark companies are generously supporting Jewish cultural and social programs in Rio and in Montevideo, Uruguay, where the Gismarks have substantial investments, going back to pre-war years.

Buenos Aires is a beautiful city. It looks like a European city with lots of parks and trees lining its streets. Between Yiddish and English, you can't get lost there, but our survivors are reluctant, scared actually, to meet with Americans or Israelis, because Argentina is still a police state. There were armed guards stationed on every floor in my hotel.

There is a very active Jewish community life, with Yiddish and Hebrew schools, a teachers' seminar, two Yiddish newspapers, a Yiddish theater and three well functioning publishing houses. I met with the editors of YIVO, *the leaders of The House of Polish Jewry, and the authors Zalman Wassertzug and Schmuel Rozanski. I was impressed with their activities, and overwhelmed by their* gastfreudlichkeit *(friendly welcome).*

I'm at my in-laws' now, and Emily and Jacob are catering to me with love and good food. Someday soon I hope to visit Panama and Honduras. Would you consider going to Panama with an old man like me?

> *Love,*
> *Sholom*

P.S. *I received a note from Esther Gismark. Her father is still holding on. Chanele adores Henrico, and calls him her savior. Wilma met a nice Jewish boy from Sao Paulo, a student at Rio University and the son of survivors. Her parents are very fond of him. Esther hopes that Wilma will get married soon and Esther wants to move to Israel. Dear Frumele, I don't know how much time you need to solve all your financial problems but my offer that you travel with me, as my companion, is a serious offer. Think about it and let me know, soon, please. S.*

ı ı ı

Dear Sol,

I visited Oscar's grave again. It was windy and the leaves were blowing. On the way home, I thought about your letter and the offer to travel with you, and I remembered when Oscar made me the same offer of travelling "as one" when he proposed to me. He did it in a funny way. We were riding in his rented car when suddenly he pointed to the fuel gauge. "This gauge shows you how much gas is left, but it is not filling the car. We need to go to a station and buy gas if we want to continue driving together, for only then will the gauge go forward."

I accepted his proposal, for by then a mutual friendship had developed between Oscar and me. We appreciated each other's company, and so we married. I felt guilty leaving the Vladeck Home in Paris, but I wanted to get away from Europe, to go to school, and become a writer. I had a suitcase full of notes and stories I had written about Smorodna, the Sisters of Mercy, and the children I had taken care of. I knew it was selfish of me to leave the children, but Europe was a

*birdcage to me, and I wanted to escape. I suppose I was try-
ing to make up for my leaving the Vladeck Home by being a
good mother and a good wife, and by working with the Jewish Labor Committee in their Children's Adoption Campaign.*

*Over the years, I did whatever I wanted to do. I at-
tended Hebrew courses at Baltimore Hebrew College and the
University of Maryland. I read books about other people's
romances.*

*Mountain climbing, cards, and scuba diving were not
for me. Yes, I had nightmares and periods of depression, especially when Oscar was working nights and I was alone. Will
we ever be able to forget the horror and the pain?*

*Secretly I began writing again. Some of my stories I
mailed to Polish and Yiddish magazines, but I'd either receive
a rejection notice, or no answer at all. Now, with Oscar gone
and the children grown, I am lonely once again. It may
sound funny for a woman to write this to a man so openly,
but I need the warm embrace of a man's arms. You were the
only man I was ever tempted to give myself to, and only my
devotion and respect for Oscar prevented me from doing so.*

*I have met some single men during the last few months
at synagogue socials and at the crowded meetings of Family
Circle, but I am bored with the small talk. Some men sound
as if they are at confession, or are being interviewed for a job.*

*The children live their own lives. Jacob works at his
father's insurance company and makes good money. He is
dating a Polish girl who works at his office. For Oscar it
would be unthinkable to let Jacob marry a* shikse *(non-Jewish girl), but after meeting Stephanie, I think she will make
him a good wife. She is willing to convert, and Jacob sounds
very happy.*

*Bernie was always a problem, studying too little and
running around too much. He likes sports, cars, and girls
who are older than he is. I know it's my fault. I spoiled him,
and now Oscar is not here to control him.*

*So, my dear Sol, my gauge shows that I am running out
of gas . . . and out of time. My running to the cemetery
doesn't do me any good. You are one of the central characters
in a novel I've just finished about our life here, our compatriots, and our benefactors, and your offer came at just the right
time. I will always remember your caring and your tenderness
when we were on our way back to Baltimore from our mission. If you still have some of this warmth and tenderness left,
I will gladly share it with you.*

Love, Frumele

*P.S. Enclosed are two of my poems, products of my secret pas-
sion to write.*

Loneliness
by Fruma Glazman

> "I shall tread, another year,
> Ways I walked with grief,
> Past the dry, ungarnered ear
> And the brittle leaf."
> *-Dorothy Parker*

The radio on the end table
has a super sensitive tone,
the music is soft and sweet,

a gentle melodious voice sings
of love and companionship:

"Jenny kissed me when we met,
Jumping from the chair she sat in.
Time, you thief! who loves to get
Sweets into your list, put that in."

I rest on the sofa, hold my
eyes closed, memories linger
of happier days more distant.
I whisper rhymes of music
I still remember the voice humming:

"Say I'm weary, say I'm sad;
Say that health has missed me;
Say I'm growing old, but add —
Jenny loved me and kissed me."

I lie on the sofa, hoping for his
image to tip-toe into the room,
he will seat himself at the edge
next to me and will gently say:
I miss you. Together we will sing:

"Say I'm weary, say I'm sad;
Say that wealth has missed me,
Say I'm growing old, but add:
Jenny loved me and kissed me."

The Widow
by Fruma Glazman

> "The voice of the dead was
> a living voice in me."
> *-Alfred Lord Tennyson*

The sun shines bright and gentle,
Yet my days are dim and gloomy.
I know that Oscar passed away, but
I can't believe that he is really gone.

> His death created an emptiness in
> my soul, an eclipse that darkened
> every spark of brightness. It left
> a deep scar that torments my heart.

I'm longing to ring out this vacuum,
pluck out the weeds of pain and hurt,
ring in some hope, peace of mind, but
his beloved voice keeps coming back.

> There are flowers on his grave, birds
> sing songs, sunlight around his tomb,
> but in my heart is a cold, windy winter,
> sadness and sorrow penetrate my soul.

This sorrowful mood continues to dim
my days, makes my heart swell with pain.
I would give my life for one day with him,
but he is gone forever. I miss him so.

◆ ◆ ◆

My dear Frumele,

Thank you for sharing your two poems with me. They give me an insight into the depths of your soul. They are a mirror of your deepest emotions and thoughts.

Your letter made me very, very happy. I miss my Bettsie as you miss your Oscar. They both gave us precious years, and the time we shared with them will always linger in our memories just as the sadness of the Holocaust will never leave us.

From a letter which I received from you a long time ago, and which I still have, I knew that you liked to write, but I didn't know that you've written a novel. I'm sure it must be a book of significance, your relating our past and your life experiences. People with talent to write, especially those few of us who are survivors, have an obligation to bear witness, to divulge everything we remember. I, myself, can't write. I make many grievous grammatical errors and misspell many words. For this, alone, I want to be with you. We will speak Yiddish as we used to in Smorodna.

I can't wait until Sunday morning, to come home, to take you in my arms and say," Frumele, Ich hob dich lieb... *Marry me. I will love you forever.*

Sholom

♦ ♦ ♦

Dearest Felicia,

Let me take this opportunity to express our most sincere appreciation for you and Sandra's donation to our Childrens Home.

Words cannot express my feelings of sympathy for the sad and cruel experiences of Sandra and her late hus-

*band. Not all that are confined in mental hospitals are men-
tally ill, but many, many on the loose are insane. . . . They
walk around us and preach prejudice, instead of understand-
ing and love.*

*There is a touch of madness in all of us, it depends how we
use it. Sandra asked me not to send her any thank you letters.
Still, I like you to know that Sandra's and your donations
were the largest we received in many years.*

*Our Church, our government support us, as you can see
from the enclosed pictures, our children look good — thanks
the Lord. But with the inflation in Poland and the large
number of disabled children we really need the support from
friends abroad. We do receive letters and donations from
many of the children who were with us and were saved, by
the grace of our Lord. They live now in Canada, Israel,
United States and Australia.*

*I asked Sandra to come and visit us, she answered that
she rather use the money it cost to travel for giving support to
institutions like ours. . . . People like Sandra and you are
encouraging us to go on doing the Lord's work.*

*My prayers and best regards to your family and Sandra.
May the Lord bless you all.*

Please, write soon.

Yours, Zoshia

Dear Sister Zoshia,

*Thank you for your letter and the picture of the chil-
dren; they look so precious. Your letters are a delight to receive. I only wish you would write more often. For many
years I had lost faith in humanity, and your actions restored
my trust. I have the strongest feelings of friendship for you.*

Every time I feel lonely or depressed, I open my notebook and read my notes about you and my mood immediately improves. Some memories are unpleasant and alienating, but when it comes to reading about you, that provides a fountain of hope and encouragement for me to go on.

Still, I am tormented by gnawing questions. The injustice done to millions of children during the war . . . where was the world? Where was God? I can't find an answer for the annihilation of millions of children, and I think I will never find an answer.

You asked me what I am doing with my free time. After almost three decades, I am back in school. I feel that I can still be useful as a nursing assistant in a nursing home here. I don't need the money, but it's a way for me to give back to the community for the opportunity they gave me to live here in freedom. I'm studying geriatric health issues at the Johns Hopkins School of Nursing. My focus is on the direct relationship between increasing age and infections like pneumonia, influenza, and tuberculosis.

I'm learning many new things in infection prevention, revaccination of the elderly with influenza vaccines, and infection control. While I worked at the Levindale Hebrew Home, I noticed that many residents suffer from osteoporosis, bone loss that comes from reduced bone strength, which leads to fractures. I registered for a course on osteoporosis and fractures for the spring semester. It's better than just sitting home feeling sorry for myself or watching television.

Nights, when I'm unable to sleep, I read books on caring for the elderly, and take notes, and I've become active, one night a month, in the local division of the American Heart Association. Americans spend a billion dollars a year on popcorn, and seven hundred million dollars a year on peanuts, but only five hundred million on heart research. Nearly one million Americans living today were born with heart defects, and one American dies every sixty-two seconds from a heart attack. Even in this country, there is a shortage of trained medical personnel to help them.

If you can get a travel permit and a visa to come to visit us, I will send you the plane tickets through Orbis Travel Agency. I'm enclosing two money orders, one for your Children's Home, and one for you, personally, to buy gifts for your Stefan and his family. I call them regularly, and enjoy talking with them. I am really looking forward to your visit. Then we can talk some more.

Yours, Felicia

31

ON HIS WAY TO FRUMELE, Sholom stopped at the Liberty Road Shopping Center for flowers. It occurred to him that there were some feelings and emotions that die, while the love he had for Frumele was very much alive.

Sometimes it is not exactly a misunderstanding or an argument that changes the yearnings or emotions; it is not circumstances or wars that diminish feelings and longings. He was thinking of Chanele. The memory of her effectually existed all those years. Who would have guessed that she was alive, that she had survived this protracted life-or-death situation? He lived with the dreadful memories of her disappearance for so many years, hoping and waiting to find her.

Yet, when he married Bettsie, he felt that he had betrayed Chanele. He loved Bettsie, but in his dreams he clung continually to the vision of Chanele, the girl with pigtails, singing, dancing, and laughing. He was astounded to find her and astonished to discover how reality, time, and circumstances had changed this vision. The gap of the years of separation was wide and deep.

He did not condemn her for marrying a German. To Chanele, her husband, Henrico, was a hero, a man worth sacrificing her life for, as he had risked his life and fortune to save her. What hurt him was to see her escaping from everything Jewish, isolating herself from her compatriots, cutting ties with the few relatives who survived.

He compared Frumele with Chanele, as he had often done in the past. Frumele also lived as a Christian, under an assumed name, among nuns, and there was the possibility that she would be swept into Christianity. The nuns were exceptionally good to her and to the children they saved from a daily danger of being discovered. Still, Frumele, with no background in religious education, came back to her people. She underwent an overwhelming change in her thinking and in her beliefs, and dedicated herself whole-heartedly to helping her compatriots, the survivors of the Holocaust.

Frumele also was dedicated to a man who had saved her life. She shared with Sholom some of her poems about her depression and thoughts of suicide after liberation. Oscar saved her and gave her a new life in freedom. Did she really love him? She was so much younger than he, and they were from very different backgrounds. He was a middle-class intellectual and she came from a socialist, proletariat environment. Yet, there was harmony, mutual respect, caring for each other, and love for their children, and so their relationship grew to be ideal.

Frumele was a model of a devoted spouse and mother. She was a skillful conversationalist, fund raiser, and, it turned out, a talented writer, although her efforts failed to be published. She was too humble and shy; what she needed was an agent, a literary mentor with an ear for poetry. Writing was for her second nature, but of secondary importance. Oscar's health, the children, and her compatriots here and in Israel were her first concern.

Another thought crossed his mind. If Henrico Gismark, so very ill, were to die today, God forbid, and Chanele, the so-very-rich widow, were to ask him to marry her, would he do it? The answer was easier than he thought: NO! Would he help her children, Wilma and Esther, in any way he could? Absolutely. And then he realized that the only woman he really cared about, and truly loved, was Frumele.

♦ ♦ ♦

Bernie opened the door and greeted Sholom with a warm handshake, "Good morning, Mr. Schwartzman," he burst into a broad smile, "Mom told me all about it." He gave Sholom a rakish wink, "You're made for each other. *Mazel Tov!*"

Frumele came to the front room and Sholom clasped her in his arms. For a moment no one said anything. They didn't need to. He just held her in his arms as he did at the forest cemetery in Smorodna, during their mission to Poland.

"My God, where did you buy flowers on Sunday morning?"

"I was planning to propose to you this morning, but I don't have a ring for you yet, so I brought flowers."

"According to Emily Post, you're supposed to get down on one knee when you propose."

"Let's seal our decision with a kiss." He drew her close, feeling her warmth.

"Sol, Bernie is in the kitchen."

"I know, but he knows that we'll be together for the rest of our lives."

Bernie came in. "I made some fresh coffee, and the bagels and lox are on the table. You two lovers go get something to eat. I've got to leave. Good luck, Mom and Sol. May I call you Sol?"

"Of course."

While they sat in the kitchen with their coffee, Sholom took a deep breath and told Frumele that he'd changed his mind about going to Panama. "I found this letter when I got home this morning. You read it out loud, and let me listen to it. It's from Eve."

Shalom, Abba (Father),

Where are all of you? I called twice, morning and evening, and had no answer. What's worse than an unanswered phone call? Two unanswered phone calls. It's urgent that I talk to you.

This letter has good and bad news. Let me start with the unpleasant news first. I'm not happy with my rented room. It is not the three floors of steps to walk up in the dark (on every floor you have to push a button to light up the next floor). It's not the people from whom I rent my room (they're hardly ever home.) It's the next-door neighbors and their dog that barks all night. I've got a lot of homework, with pages of reading every night, and I can't concentrate. Besides, I need my sleep. I've tried to stuff my ears with cotton, but it doesn't help. I found a room with an elderly couple in a villa not far from the Technion, and someone who can drive me home after classes, so I don't have to wait for the overloaded Egged Bus. But, Abba, I need money. I can't ask the people where I live now to return the rent money which I paid in advance for the full semester. They spent it when they painted my room and put in a new bed and desk.

And now the good news. I met Aviel, a third-year student at Technion. He is tall (6'4"), dark and handsome, and speaks fluent French, English and Arabic. He corrects my Hebrew and I, his English. He's served three years already in Zahal (the Israeli Armed Forces, or IDF), and is now in the Reserves. He's a tankist, that's all I know. The Israelis are very secretive about their military service, especially with foreigners.

But here's the problem. He is Dati (religious). He wears a kippah (skullcap) and says prayers before and after he eats. His parents are Israeli-born Sephardim. His father is an instructor at the ORT school here; Aviel graduated from the ORT Technical School in Haifa before he went into the army. His mother works in the Bank Mizrachi as an investment consultant. His grandparents live just two blocks from their house. His grandfather owns a jewelry store in downtown Haifa, and is a craftsman of religious objects. His grandmother, a retired teacher, helps part-time in the store. Theirs is a large family. All the children are married, and they live all over Israel. I was invited to a Friday night dinner; it was a very long walk from my room, but it was worth it. Dinner lasted for two full hours. Not only do they serve many dishes (no gefilte fish), but between dishes they sing Zmiroth (Shabbat songs) and they talk and ask lots of questions. At first I felt like I was being interrogated, but really they made me feel like I was at home. They wanted to know about you and Mom. When I told them that my mother passed away, and I became emotional, they stopped asking me questions. Later, we all went up on the roof and Aviel's mother served tea and fruit.

Then Aviel and his father disappeared for some discussions in their huge library. When he finally came out, he told me that he was ready to walk me back to my room. His parents wished me Shabbat Shalom, and invited me to come again for Shabbat dinner next week.

Aviel*'s* mother, wearing a long, multi-colored Shabbat dress and matching scarf to cover her hair, walked with us to the first corner. She hugged me and thanked me for "enhancing her Shabbat table."

Aviel walked beside me, taking my arm to help me cross the poorly lit streets. He told me that his father liked me, and approved of me, but had warned Aviel not to hurt my feelings because I am a Yetomah (an orphan). He told Aviel that he could not propose to me until he had first spoken to you, Abba. Aviel's father called me Bachura adina (a gentle girl), and Aviel told me that he loves me very much. He said that if I need a new place to live, he could find me a room in his grandfather's villa. The room would have a separate entrance, but it needs furnishing (a new bed and mattress, etc.)

So, dear Abba, I hope you can come to see us. Please bring a letter from our Rabbi, stating that I have never been married. The Rabbanut (the Rabbinical Authority) here demands this proof. My love to Jimmie and Lorna. I wish Lorna would come here. We need good teachers. Please call me as soon as you receive this letter. Aviel sends his greetings.

Love, and L'hitraot, Chava (Eve)

♦ ♦ ♦

Frumele paused for a moment and then said, "It's sad that Bettsie is not alive to read this letter. I'm happy for you and Eve. I wish Bernie would go to Israel and meet a nice girl there. Sol, if you want me to, I'll go with you, but if

Aviel's parents are Orthodox and it will be embarrassing for them, and for you, if we come together, stay in the same hotel, come to their home."

"Your point is well taken. Let's get married."

Frumele got up, but didn't say anything. Sholom followed her. "You haven't answered me."

"I was thinking about the timing. Isn't it a bit too early? People will talk."

"People will talk anyhow. It's what we feel is right, what's good, for us and for our children. That's what counts."

Frumele turned her face towards his. Sholom ran his fingers against her smooth skin. She threw her arms around him and said, "I'm ready to marry you any time you say!"

"Which Rabbi shall I call? Rosenblatt? Herzberg?"

"I like Herzberg."

"Shall I call him now?"

"Wait," she said, and threw herself into his arms and kissed him intensely, tenderly, happy as a teenager after her first kiss. Frumele beamed, "Oh, Sol, it's been such a long time."

"For me, too."

32

My dear friend, Herman,

What a small world. Do you remember Yitzhak Ginzburg, the director of the Ben Ari Museum at Bat Yam? On a visit to Silver Spring I met him and his wife, Lida, in the home of mutual friends, Helen and Abraham Goldkind.

The Ginzburgs invited us to visit their son Yankel's home in Chevy Chase, where we met Yankel, his wife, Pamela, and their son, Aviel.

We spent the whole evening sharing memories about Poland, Sister Zoshia, and about our present lives. I was so impressed with Yankel's art, and with the whole family, really, that I wrote this poem about our visit. I couldn't help but think of the million and a half Jewish children who perished in the Holocaust, and wonder how many Yankel Ginzburgs were among them. . . .

Yankel and his art are testimony to the living spirit of our people. As Aaron Zeitlin said, "We are going on to live and create, despite all despites."

I hope you will approve of my poem about this great artist and his family.

Art and the Artist
        for Yankel Ginzburg

Art like nature, its course,
come from the same source,
an artist's planned play,
for people to enjoy.
            No training is required
            to be admired and inspired,
            by the demonstrations
            of your artistic creations.
Art's perfection was unknown
for me, but with my own
vision, spiritual intuition,
I absorbed your compositions.
            Art like nature, is intermingled,
            it can't be separately singled
            out, to fit the viewer's desire,
            or to what the astists aspire.
Your paintings and sculptures,
serve all nations and cultures,
we enjoy your art like a feat
that make our life sweet.

♦ ♦ ♦

Dear Herman,

This letter comes to you from Switzerland. On the way home from Israel, we stopped for a week to rest at a resort on Lake Geneva. Switzerland is one of the most beautiful countries I've ever seen. It is a classic tourist country, with a mighty stream of people from all over the world. At our age, it is difficult for us to visit the snow-covered glaciers, but we enjoy the view of the permanently snow-topped mountains and the lakes and valleys between Lake Geneva and Lake Constance. The people here speak French, Italian, and a German that almost sounds like Galician Yiddish.

We visited Chanele and Henrico Gismark. They have a small home in the Rhone Valley, very near a beautiful old castle. Chanele pushes him in his wheelchair, and they live only for each other. They don't go out much in public, and Henrico refuses to visit Germany. He depends on his sister, Gertrude, to take care of the affairs of their parents' estate there.

The Gismarks are very generous people. When I told them about my war experiences and about Sister Zoshia, Henrico asked me for the address of the Children's Home in Lodz. He promised to send a substantial donation to the Home, in honor of Sister Zoshia.

Their daughter, Esther, is a student at Columbia University in New York. She is visiting her parents now with her fiance, Eli, a student at the Jewish Theological Seminary. They plan to move to Israel after they both graduate. Esther has already been offered a job as a language instructor at Tel Aviv University. She is fluent in Portuguese, German, English, and Spanish, and she speaks Hebrew like a pro.

Henrico and Chanele invited us to come and stay with them in Rio this winter (their summer), but Sholom politely declined. He has changed lately. As busy and involved as he was in the Baltimore community before our marriage, so has he become withdrawn and totally disconnected lately.

So, now it is Jacob and his wife, Sarah, who have become active in the Young Leadership of the Associated Jewish Charities, Israel Bonds, and the Talmudical Academy. Shalom

*prefers to stay home, with his Yiddish newspapers and books
and magazines. Our children seldom call, but we still get
together for the holidays and the birthdays of our grandchildren, Oscar and Bettsie.*

*Bernie finally got tired of fooling around and settled
down with Bobbie, the daughter of Sholom's close friend, Joseph Klein. They seem to be very happy. They kiss and hug in
our presence, and Bobbie's dream is to become a mother. She
loves Jacob and Sarah's children, but Bernie is in no hurry.
Lorna teaches and lives in Pikesville. She shares a condo-
minium with a nice, young woman. I don't know about
Lorna, but her roommate is definitely a lesbian. The only*
nachas *(joy) Sholom has now is from his Chavele (Eve),
Aviel, and their two boys, Joinele and Lazar.*

*Bettsie's parents are the most wonderful people. Sholom
calls them every week, and they talk about the children.
Sholom became more observant. He says* Kaddish *for his father and the people of Smorodna every time we go to synagogue.*

*I'm still in touch with Sister Zoshia. After the collapse of
communism in Poland, her brother, Stefan, and his family
returned to Lodz, but they came back after six months. It was
a good thing that they didn't sell their home in Bowie.*

*The Rotstein Family Circle is now only a fraction of
what it used to be. We only get together on* Chanukkah *and*
Purim. *Some of our older compatriots have passed away or
moved to Florida. In the summer, many of them go to Ocean
City. I tried talking Sholom into moving to Florida, but he
refuses. Cards don't interest him, and the sun gives him a
headache. Probably if we were to move somewhere, it would
be to Haifa.*

Jimmie is now a full partner in a prestigious law firm in

Washington, DC. He does a lot of travelling, mostly in South America, so we rarely see him.

I love Baltimore, its people, its institutions, and our new downtown, but with all my activities at Levindale, I long for a vacation somewhere like Florida.

So much for family matters. As for my writings, I gave up trying to find an agent or a publisher for my stories and memoirs, but I still think, for some future historian, that my notes have some value, especially for our children and for our Smorodna compatriots.

As soon as we return from Switzerland, I will personally deliver all my notes to the archives of the United States Holocaust Memorial Museum in Washington for safekeeping. Sholom sends his regards to Susi and you.

In friendship, Frumele

Epilogue

I'm amazed, when looking into my past and travelling in Israel, to discover incidents relating to by-gone years and to our landsmen. When memory wells go dry, a visit to the places we visited almost three decades ago click into place and plug into the story, recalling some particular experiences, and they emerge, like cocoons, caterpillars changing into butter-flies.

Our visit to Israel revealed the unexpectedness of life. From our shtetl, our childhood, and that grim war, the focus of our lives, because of our children, grandchildren, and now a great grandchild, has turned to hope and faith. We have discovered a new, continuing relationship with our children and our people. We are no longer tourists or visitors, pilgrims or lonely wayfarers, but family who have reclaimed our iden-tity, our roots, and full control of our lives.

With all the freedom and human goodness we found in Baltimore, the old and new friends, our preoccupation with the welfare of our community, Jewish activities, and our con-cerns and activities with the rest of the city, we still searched for roots and for meaning in life. We travelled all over the world like Sholom Aleichem's "Astrayed Stars." Like the Legend of the Wandering Jew, we were fascinated with the places we visited and the people we met. We established new relationships and friendships with men and women of many nations and races, and we came to the conclusion that we were just like everyone else, but something was missing — besides the gruesome yesterdays, there was no vision of hope for tomorrow.

While we wandered over Europe, and North and South America, we met many Biblical Cains, eternal wanderers, killers and haters of their own brothers and sisters. They don't wear the mark put on them by God as the story appears in the Bible, but their souls, their words, and the look in their eyes still carry the load of hatred on their shaven heads.

We met other versions of wanderers, Jews, and Christians who believe in a better world, in peace and harmony among nations. They preach and teach about peace on Earth, despite the death and destruction that roams our world, from Bosnia to Haiti, from Rwanda to Sudan, from Yemen to Somalia, the hatred of one people for another.

I look back on our lives a half century ago, at the silence of the world's leaders during the Holocaust, and compare that to the indifference of today's leaders for the suffering in the world. When evil, the killing of innocent people, goes unpunished, and our all-powerful God is Himself wandering in exile — He's in churches, temples, and synagogues — He is absent from the homes and the hearts of His people. I've come to the conclusion, not that I am a repentant sinner, not that I am God's favorite child, but that I am responsible for this world by protecting the assets of freedom, equality, and love for our fellow man, by carrying it on my not-so-strong, old shoulders.

I am tempted to accept God, His (or Her) omnipotence, as long as He will support me in my ideas, my pleasant fantasies, that real peace, freedom, and harmony among people are possible. I don't know if I can stop the genocide in Rwanda or Bosnia. Our own government shows impotence and is reluctant to stop the killings between the Hutus and the Tutsi tribes, but doing nothing is repeating the crimes of silence of the Holocaust.

My father was a liberal socialist, a member of the Bund, and there were no religious observances in our home. I remember asking my father why he gave charity to our town's Rabbi Kornblitt, or his beadle, every Thursday, when he did not believe in Paradise. His response to me was that the Rabbi was a good, decent man who collected the money to help the poor, the elderly, and the sick people in our town; that this had nothing to do with religion, but was a human obligation to share with the less fortunate among us. He said that if the socialist ideas of justice and equality would prevail, there would be no need to knock on doors every Thursday to provide food for the poor among us. It would be the obligation of government, both federal and local, to take care of all peoples' needs.

I remember my father sitting home on Rosh Hashanah, reading to me and my mother what he called "Religious Myths." It was about how religions developed among wandering nomads, the Mongolians, Caucasians, and Semites, 4500 B.C. Even then, people were driven by despair for their lost way of life, and hoped to find a better life elsewhere, where food would be more plentiful and the terror of war would be no more.

He spoke of the Jewish tribes roaming the desert, fighting Amalek and other nomad marauders, their belief in a protective God and their hope of finding a fertile land, as promised to Abraham. Some Jews have sustained that hope to this day. My father considered that hope a Utopian ideal. "The fate of the Jewish people is bound with the fate of all mankind," he'd say.

I realize now how right he was. We can't isolate ourselves from the world and do nothing when children are hacked to death, when black-white hatred is preached in our universities, in our backyards, even in our churches. But my father was wrong when he left our destiny to the socialists of his time. The dreams and hopes of our people to have their own homeland, to be masters of their own destiny, has breathed new life into the remnants of the Holocaust, and we have again become a living people.

I remember my father reading to us the story of Prometheus and Pandora, how man was created from earth and divine materials. Prometheus gave man the image of God, an upright statue, so that while all animals turn their faces downward and look at the Earth, man raises his face to Heaven and gazes at the stars. I liked the part describing how the first woman was created, that Pandora was made in heaven, and every god contributed something to make her perfect. Venus gave her beauty, Mercury gave her persuasion, and Apollo gave her music. My father read "Pandora was sent to Earth in good faith by Jupiter to bless man, that she was given a box containing her marriage presents and into which every god had put some blessing. She opened the box carelessly, and all the blessings escaped, except for hope."

It seems that hope is religion and the power that sustains mankind. It is the only salvation for our world. It sustained *the children in my orphanage, in the* Klasztor, *in the Vladeck Home in Paris. I had been neurotic and helpless, fooling the children with false hopes. I remember little girls, tugging at my sleeves, asking now that the war was over, would their mommies come to take them home. I lied and filled them with false hopes that, yes, there was a possibility that their parents had survived, and Sister Zoshia did the same.*

I had placed her on a pedestal of perfection and honesty. When I was angry or upset, depressed and thinking of suicide, she spoke of hope. I was fooled, and I believed her.

Rabbi Elimelech Hertzberg, of blessed memory, did the same. When Oscar died, he came to the house, and I shared with him the myriads of complaints that were nestled in my soul. I told him that there was no space left for faith or hope.

He quoted from Job: "Why is light given to him that is in misery?"

He said that it was all right to mourn, to feel disappointment, even to feel panicky being left all alone, having lost a father-figure like Oscar, though groaning like Job would not help my situation or my children. I must recognize my own worth, and have hope.

Later, when I married Sholom, he kidded me, and even mocked me, saying that someday, through our children, or our grandchildren, we would learn to deal realistically with our past, that all our childhood confusions would solve themselves, not by his advice, but by situations that we'd face on our own. Every experience, every happening, would dominate and strengthen our faith, our roots, and our hope.

I was thinking of all this, these bits and pieces of our past, at a Bris *at Sholom's grandchildren's synagogue in Israel. Chavele's oldest son, Joinele, and his wife, Chamutal, became*

*the proud parents of a seven-pound four-ounce bundle of joy,
and they named him Ohr Yehuda. They live in Carmiel, a
new town of 35,000 people from all over the world, in Galil.
The young couple live in an humble garden apartment which
is beautifully furnished. Their garden, with its lovely flowers,
looks like a picture-perfect postcard.*

Chamutal comes from a very religious family, and the
Bris *took place on* Shavuot, *the Pentecost holiday marking
the giving of the Torah to the Jews, and celebrating the gathering of the first fruits. But the party took place the day after*
Shavuot. *One hundred and twenty people came for music,
dancing, speeches, and good food. Sholom, the great-grandfa-
ther, was singing and dancing, and happier than I've ever
seen him. Joinele is a Chaplain in the Israeli army, and many
of the guests were chaplains and rabbis who came from all
over Israel.*

*Chavele insisted that we come with her to visit the Beth
Lochamei Hagetaot (The Ghetto Fighters House) between
Akko (Acre) and Naharia. The kibbutz was built by the living witnesses to the mass destruction of thousands of Jewish
communities. Nearly all of the founders came from Poland
and Lithuania, survivors of the ghettoes and camps, partici-
pants in the Jewish resistance movements, partisans, or soldiers in the Allied armies. The museum is dedicated to the
memory of Yitzhak Katzenelson, the great, tragic poet whose
lamentations for the suffering of the Jewish people made him
a true elegist of the Holocaust. I was privileged to know him
when I studied in Lodz, Poland, before the war. Yitzhak
Katzenelson perished in Auschwitz in the beginning of May,
1944. Sholom and I contribute regularly to the Ghetto Fighters House for their worthwhile projects dealing with the*

teaching of martyrdom and resistance.

Chavele wanted us to see the new addition to the museum, Yad Layeled — a Children's Memorial commemorating a million and a half Jewish children who perished in the Holocaust.

The Memorial was designed by the architect, Ram Carmi, who co-designed the Supreme Court building in Jerusalem. Chavele worked for this firm for many years and this new Memorial Museum is for her a way to remember the children of Smorodna who perished in Europe.

We walked around the the new buildings which are in an advanced stage of completion with Simcha Stein, the Executive Director of the Ghetto Fighters' House. While he pointed out to us the eternal light, the stained glass windows, designed by Roman and Ardyn Halter, suggested by children's drawings from Theresenstadt, the Janusz Korchak exhibition and the Childrens' Hall, I was thinking of my own children in Helenuwek, in the Klasztor, and the remnants of the children saved in the Vladeck Home in Paris. I was thinking of my parents, who raised me in the spirit of love for humanity and in my mind emerged a poem, or was it a song I heard many years ago written by a Yiddish poet?

"All the world's children are my brothers and sisters,
but all Jewish children are my own . . . "

Fifty years ago the Jewish Labor Committee, the Workmen's Circle, and the labor unions adopted and saved the remnants of the children who survived the calamity of the Holocaust. Now, fifty years later, Sholom's daughter, a second generation survivor, Workmen's Circle of America and many first, second, and third generation survivors were building a monument for children to learn about those children who perished in Europe. Simcha Stein told us about Vladka and Benjamin Meed and Joseph Mlotek, survivors of the Warsaw Ghetto, who are trying their utmost to finish this Yad L'Yeled project.

From the Ghetto Fighters House we travelled to Kibbutz Gesher Haziv, where children of our Smorodna landsleit and many youth from Baltimore live. We heard the sad news that Mike Duvdevani, one of the founders of the kibbutz, passed away last year. Of all our Smorodna landsleit, only one elderly woman is still living on the kibbutz. Her children and grandchildren are active in the kibbutz, and in the political life of the country, but they know very little about Smorodna, and their family's life there. Their concern is for the future, peace with their Arab neighbors, water rights, roads, housing, schools, absorption of the new immigrants, and the economy.

We visited Kiryat Siegal in Ramat Gan. It looks like a town for senior citizens. Our Smorodna-sponsored building is still standing, but it could use gallons of paint, inside and out, and some walls need to be repaired. Alas, we could not find any Smorodna compatriots. Some had passed away, and some were in old age homes in B'nai B'rak and Natania.

We met Chanele Gismark who was visiting her daughter, Esther, Esther's husband Eli, and their four boys. They live in northern Judea, and the children study in yeshivot in Jerusalem. Eli is a licensed tour guide for groups who speak Spanish, Portuguese, German, Hebrew, and English. We found Chanele and Esther at Yad Vashem, in the Valley of the Destroyed Communities, a monument designed to commemorate the five thousand Jewish communities in Europe destroyed during World War II by the Nazis and their collaborators.

*We walked around the massive stones searching for
Smorodna, but could not find it. We looked for Dr. Yitzhak
Arad, the Chairman of Yad Vashem Directorate, and were
told that he had retired, and was now teaching in the United
States. We finally found the new director of the Valley of the
Destroyed Communities, Mr. Eli Dlin, who promised to rec-
tify the omission and add Smorodna to the memorials of the
destroyed Jewish communities of Poland.*

*So, all that is left of Smorodna are memories, the name
of our town inscribed on a square stone, and the names of
our loved ones who perished, carried now by our grandchildren in America and in Israel, where our children live.*

*We are back home in Baltimore, and Sholom is back at
work in his synagogue. He volunteers at the Associated Jewish
Charities, and enjoys studying Yiddish and Hebrew at the
Baltimore Hebrew University. His health is failing, but he
savors every day as a blessing from God. Every letter from
Israel, the good and the bad, he accepts as natural, as part of
life, as reality, and he has complete faith and hope for the
future.*

*I'm volunteering again at the Levindale Nursing Home,
and, from time to time, I call the few remaining Smorodna
landsleit in Baltimore and Washington. We see each other
only at the city-wide Yom HaShoah Memorial Service, or
when someone has died. We hide away, out of sight from our
own people.*

*The darkness of the past is still all around me, after fifty
years. My father and mother, and Oscar and Sister Zoshia
are still in my dreams. I dream about a more gentle world,
where people are more concerned with, and sympathetic to,
the needs of others, and are willing to share, to reach out, and*

build a better world for everyone. So, in this darkness (liter-
ally, because I have glaucoma), I see sparks of light. I see
hope.

Frumele

♦ ♦ ♦

Dear Frumele,

I get particular pleasure reading your letters and the
manuscript of your novel, My Baltimore Landsmen. *You see,*
I am one of the former Baltimoreans who knew all the people
you write about, the distinguished rabbis, the community
leaders, the survivors you interviewed and taped, and some of
the characters you created.

I understand your high regard and admiration for Sister
Zoshia as I can apprehend Chanele Goratski's fervent love for
her husband, Hans — Henrico. But, with all the Righteous
Gentiles in the Alley of Christian Heroism at Yad Vashem in
Jerusalem, with all the brave people of Italy, Denmark, Swe-
den, and other countries in Europe, with all the Zegota's and
Schindler's Lists, the Jan Karski's and Raoul Wallenbergs, the
fact remains that six million of our people were abandoned by
the world's leaders, by their neighbors, and were murdered by
the Germans and their helpers. We Jews have a strong
memory — we remember Amalek and we pay homage to the
Sister Zoshias — but we must not for one moment forget that
for every Jewish child saved, thousands of innocent Jewish
children were murdered. In every country in Europe, there
were collaborators —Vlasovcy, Quislings, Iron Guards,
Ustashis, Lithuanians, and Ukrainian volunteers, as well as
millions of silent bystanders, who helped to make Europe
"Judenrein."

Sister Zoshia is a spark of light in the current darkness in the world around us. Your novel is about our landsleit — yours and mine — and their rescuers, about the good people of Baltimore, Maryland, who gave us an opportunity to start new lives in freedom and hope for a better future.

But, who speaks for the millions who perished? . . . for the 5,000 obliterated Jewish communities in Europe? Who speaks for the Gypsies, Russians, Poles, the partisans, allied soldiers, prisoners of war, dissidents, homosexuals, and the handicapped?

So, my dear Frumele, yours is only part of a story, an episode, a page in the tragic chapter of our past. We must all continue to tell our stories and especially the story of Jewish children. Elie Wiesel wrote me after I shared your letter about your visit to Kibbutz Lohamey Hagetaot and the new Yad L'Yeled Museum, "What they have seen, God himself has not seen. Their story of ultimate helplessness remains to be told. Because of them we are moved to despair; because of them we must overcome despair."

You write about hope. Without decisive action, hope is just a colorful soap bubble. Only decisions, participation in matters of concern, are the alternatives for hope.

Faith, dreams, hopes without action, without facing reality and joining in the universal struggle for a better tomorrow for humanity, for everlasting peace, for human rights, for freedom from fear and bigotry, the word HOPE will remain an empty vocable. It is our obligation to keep alive the memories of the past, we must teach our children an everlasting principle: Not knowing everything about our past is no disgrace. But, being silent, indifferent, to what happens around us today, is a crime. Your observations written during your years in the Klasztor are a mixture of wit and venom. We all lived surrounded by venom, by beasts with PhD's who built crematorias and gas chambers, developed the most systematic killing on earth. Whatever it was, wit or destiny, sheer coincidence or fate, I bless the hour when you and your landsmen were saved.

Herman Taube

About the Author

Since he arrived in the United States in 1947, Herman Taube has written for numbers of newspapers, including the *Jewish Daily Forward*, *The Jewish Week* (Washington, D.C.), and the *Algemeiner Journal* (Brooklyn, New York). He has written numbers of books, the most recent *Land of Blue Skies*; *Between the Shadows: New & Selected Works*; *Autumn Travels, Devious Paths*; and *Kyzyl Kishlak — Refugee Village*. A graduate of American University with an M.A. in Literature-Creative Writing, he lectures regularly on Yiddish Literature, World War II and the Holocaust. He has taught at the University of Maryland and The American University and is currently a faculty member at the College of Jewish Studies — Board of Jewish Education. At present, he is White House correspondent for the *Jewish Forward*. Taube serves on the board of the Days of Remembrance Committee of the U.S. Holocaust Memorial Museum.